MANHATTAN BOMBSHELL

Reporter Larry O'Halloran has got himself a great scoop. So he's shocked when his editor refuses to run it — and no rival newspaper will touch it, either. It seems the press in this city is caught in a stranglehold, scared to print the truth, fearing retribution from a mysterious figure named 'the Raven'. So Larry starts his own paper, the *Manhattan Bombshell*, printing the stories no other sheet dares to. But the Raven will make him pay for his audacity . . .

Books by Norman Firth
in the Linford Mystery Library:

NORMAN FIRTH

◆

MANHATTAN BOMBSHELL

Complete and Unabridged

LINFORD
Leicester

First published in Great Britain

First Linford Edition
published 2018

A catalogue record for this book is available
from the British Library.

ISBN 978–1–4448–3762–9

Published by
F. A. Thorpe (Publishing)
Anstey, Leicestershire

Set by Words & Graphics Ltd.
Anstey, Leicestershire
Printed and bound in Great Britain by
T. J. International Ltd., Padstow, Cornwall

This book is printed on acid-free paper

1

It all started that day I walked into the city editor's office with the hottest story Manhattan had ever read. I slapped it in front of him, said, not without a certain amount of airy conceit: 'There it is, Chief — print it!'

He glowered at me over the top of his rimless spectacles, shifted the green shade back off his sweating forehead, and growled: 'Print what? What is it?'

'It's a sensation,' I told him, and would have added that it was also a 'scoop', except that the term had become a bit corny through too much use. 'It's the real lowdown on why Ancaster Allan committed suicide!'

He stiffened at that, and I could see I'd got him right where he lived. He picked the copy up and glanced over it; he didn't speak until he'd finished reading, then he said: 'You sure of your facts?'

'I always am,' I asserted. 'You know

that. When did I ever make slips during all my seven years on this sheet?'

He couldn't tell me, because I never had. But he didn't seem pleased about the copy. I got annoyed, said: 'Well?'

He threw it down on the desk, and I nearly threw a swoon when he rapped: 'We can't use it, O'Halloran.'

'But . . . '

'Don't argue. We can't print it! And if you'll take my advice you'll head right out to where there's a fire, and *burn* it piece by piece. Get me?'

'I'm damned if I do,' I said, forgetting his position. 'You employ me on this rag to get news, don't you? Okay, well, *that's* news! Nobody knows just why Ancaster Allan committed suicide: all the other sheets printed the mere details of his death. I go out and get the real lowdown for you, and what happens?'

'I tell you we can't print it,' he said, coolly.

'You're darned right you do — and what I want to know is, *why*? Why can't you print it? Whose toes would you be treading on?'

'I'll tell you something,' he informed me, gravely. 'Speaking about toes — if you don't lay off this story, you're liable to be found in the morgue with yours turned up one of these days! How come you got the story?'

'His dame,' I said. 'She gave it me. Didn't want her name mentioning. But what I want to know is why you can't run it.'

He shook his bald head and hauled his shade over his eyes; he said, shortly: 'We can't. For the simple reason that we've had instructions from the owner of the sheet to print nothing about Ancaster Allan, other than the usual obituary. Now blow, and take your dynamite with you!'

'No you don't,' I growled, waving the copy at him. 'I still want to know why it's being covered up. When a well-known stage star like Ancaster Allan ups and shoots himself for no good reason that anybody knows — and when I go to the trouble of taking his ritzy momma out to the night-spots to get the lowdown on the affair — and then you refuse to print it, I definitely require to know why not! Allan was being blackmailed — more than he

3

could afford to pay. I found that out, and it's all down there. Why won't you run it?'

He sighed, said: 'Far as the expense you've run is concerned, you can pick up that amount from the cashier. I'll okay a slip for you.'

'It isn't the expense,' I snorted, and I was feeling plenty riled what with one thing and another. This was the sixth good story I'd brought in in two months — and every one had been unceremoniously squashed! I was beginning to wonder what was at back of it!

'Look here, son,' he said kindly. 'Just lay off anything which is bad medicine, will you? Take my say-so that this is poison. Dump it!'

'Like hell I will!' The Irish in me was getting as savage as the devil. I wanted to know why I was being edited out of existence — maybe the city had a grudge against me — maybe he didn't want my stuff to go through. I went on: 'You may be the big oyster round here, but I'm telling you this; I figure if a story's got news value, like in this case, it should run. Now — and I'm giving it you square

— either you print this, or else . . . '

'Or else *what*, O'Halloran?' he says, raising his brows.

'Or else you can accept my notice to take effect immediately,' I snapped back at him.

And just like that he said: 'Okay. Pick up your paycheque on the way out!'

I'm not saying I actually staggered, but I remember clutching the arm of a chair for support. I stuttered: 'Hey — what — ?'

'You said it, didn't you?'

'Yeah, but you damn well can't afford to lose *me*! Look at the stuff I've brought you in . . . '

'You have,' he granted. 'Brought in fine stuff. But you know you were told to lay off certain stories lately, don't you? So were all the other sheets . . . and you had to be stubborn and go your own way, finding things out. Okay — now you kick because we won't print 'em! You resign — I accept. And then you want to kick because I haven't beefed about it. What d'you want me to do, O'Halloran? Go on my knees an' beg you to stick for the sake of your grey-haired old editor-in-chief?

Nix! You can get. I can't hit my knees anyway — troubled with rheumatism. Goodbye, son.'

He did it to me just like that; and then he went on correcting proofs without even bothering to watch me high-tail out of the office. I grabbed my copy; I said: 'Okay, you heel. I guess you've got some reason for keeping this stuff out . . . '

'So have all the other editors in town,' he acknowledged. 'And the reason is we don't want to lose our jobs. We've got our set instructions from the owners — I admit your story's great, and I would like to give it front page with banners. But I can't. I daren't, if you want it plainer. I got a wife and four kids that need to eat, and I got to see they do. Now, son, forget all this; let the whole thing drop, and go on working here on the jobs you're assigned to.'

'You can kiss my little finger,' I told him, heatedly, only I didn't say 'little finger'. 'I'm blowing. You don't want newshawks here. What you want is yes-men. There's plenty of papers aching to get me, so don't get thinking you're doing me any favours saying I can stay on if I scrap this copy. I'm hitting the trail, Chief, and I'm farming this story out to whoever'll print it. So long!'

I grabbed my hat and burned the carpet towards the door. He looked up and said: 'Larry — '

'Yeah?'

'Don't forget your paycheque.'

'You can . . . ' I began, then cursed some and left it unsaid. I couldn't blame the editor — if he had his instructions, he had them. It wasn't his fault, he was a good newspaperman; but, as he said, he'd a family to think of. I didn't, and that's why I didn't need to work anywhere where I didn't approve of the methods.

I stormed out into the street; I was so mad I could have bit lumps out of Oswald Dexter's ears, if he'd been around. Dexter was the owner of the paper I'd recently been working for, and it was he who gave the instructions as to the paper's policy. He owned some half-dozen other sheets up and down the States, and he was one of the big-time newspaper owners of the day. But big-time or not I'd have given plenty to have told him what I thought of him banning good copy like the stories of mine he'd put the hoof on lately. Yes, sir, I was good and mad!

I bust into the office of the *Clarion* later that afternoon, after I'd cooled off some. I saw Ferguson, the chief sub.

I said: 'I'm out of a job!'

He looked at me kind of funny. He said: 'Are you telling *me*?'

'Sure I'm telling you — did you know?'

'Known all afternoon. You flung your job in with the *Recorder*, didn't you?'

'I did. You know why?'

'Not rightly. Heard you sent in some copy that was too hot to run.'

'I sent in some copy — *period*,' I told him irately. 'It wasn't too hot to run — it was sensational. Exclamation mark.'

'And . . . ?'

'They wouldn't print it.' I snorted in disgust. 'So I'm out here to find a real man-sized paper that will print it. I'd like to see Gaynor.'

Gaynor was their editor-in-chief. Ferguson said: 'Sorry, no can do. You'd better blow.'

I stared at him. I said: 'What's eating you? I want to see Gaynor — I'm here to offer my services.'

'They aren't wanted, O'Halloran. Sorry, but that's a fact.'

'Why not? And how d'you know? Maybe Gaynor'll think they are. What say you got in the matter?'

'I'm telling you what Gaynor told me to tell you if you came here looking for a job, pal. He said to say you wasn't wanted.'

'Sub-edit that last sentence,' I sneered.

'Okay — he told me to tell you you were not required. Now you can go as soon as you like, Smart Alec.'

I gave him a sign with my fingers which told him what I thought of him; he moved towards me, scowling, and I shook the dust of the *Clarion* offices off my dogs. I tried the *Sentinel* next. I spoke to Gifford, the owner, there, happening to contact him as he left.

'Oh, Mr. Gifford,' I said, laying a hand on his arm. 'I want to see you . . . '

He shook it off. He said: 'It isn't mutual, O'Halloran. I'm in rather a hurry.'

I still detained him, smiling ingratiatingly. I told him: 'I've got a story that'll lift the sales of your paper into the million class . . . it's yours if you'll print it and find me a job on the *Sentinel*.'

He shook his head. 'If you mean the Ancaster Allan story you've been hawking round town all day, it's no dice, O'Halloran. Take my tip and shove that story away out of sight somewhere. You'll ruin your career with it, so help you. You *have* ruined your career with it. So long.'

I stood staring after his back; then I fumed like hell and told high heaven just what I thought of the whole stinking racket. Which was plenty.

But I kept going; I went from one office to another, and at every one I got the same story. 'No dice, O'Halloran. You're loaded with T.N.T.!'

And that's the way it still stood when I wound up at Danny's Beanery on thirty-third for a snack. I was tired, disconsolate, and inclined to sling the blasted Ancaster Allan story into the closest garbage can. But something stopped me. All the obstinacy in my nature had been roused by the opposition I'd encountered.

Newsmen are like that; after years of shoving your snoot into other folks' business, and refusing to take no for an answer, you get so that you can't turn back. Nothing shakes you. I've seen a newsman trapped under a trolley wheel, cigarette in mouth, notebook in hand, taking a statement from the driver of the trolley while he waited for the blood wagon to take him to the pre-burial factory.

So I was stubborn. And, by God, I decided I'd stay that way. If somebody unknown figured they could buy off Larry O'Halloran, they were making the biggest mistake of their lives. They couldn't. I'd print that story if it cost me my life . . .

I bumped into Dave Golman in Danny's. Golman's a fellow reporter off the *Recorder* for whom I, personally, never had much use. He's a thin, sneaky type, who dug up all the delectable bits about playboys and their new mommas. I don't like the breed — that isn't reporting, it's tittle-tattling. He lounged across and said:

11

'Hear you got kicked off the sheet, O'Halloran?'

'Then you heard wrong, snoop-nostrils,' I told him. 'I handed in my resignation, that's what. Not that it matters to you.'

He sniggered, and I got a feeling I'd like to stroke his long nose with my knuckles. He went on: 'Maybe that's the way you like to tell it, but I guess you were only one jump ahead of the chief when you resigned. If you'd waited a second he'd have fired you. You always had to go digging up stories anyone with sense would leave alone. Look where it's got you.'

I stood up. I said: 'Blow, Golman.'

He laughed again: 'Take it easy. You don't look too fresh for a reporter who's got hold of a swell story. Or maybe you've been tramping round and finding out nobody wants it — or you, now?'

'Listen,' I snarled. 'If this story doesn't hit headlines, I still won't back down. I go right straight to police headquarters and see if they're interested in it. And how d'you like that?'

He didn't like it; his face showed that.

He muttered: 'You're crazy. That'd be a fool thing to do when you know someone's at back of its suppression.'

'Sure — I know that. And I'll get whoever *is* at back of it before I'm through, watch me.'

He mumbled: 'You're nuts. I wouldn't want to be around you in the next few days — you'll carry trouble. I got to go.'

He went; he went fast. And I sat down again.

It hadn't been just loud talk, that threat of mine to go to the cops. Of course, the girl's confession wasn't worth a whole lot; it just revealed the fact that Ancaster Allan had been paying big money to prevent something about him becoming known. She hadn't been able to tell me who the person behind it was, or what it was he'd wanted hidden up. But I had a feeling that she knew more — that she could tell me plenty — *plenty*!

If I hung around some more, I'd get to know. Meanwhile, I had the signed statement from her in my pocket, and if the cops didn't rouse themselves when they saw that, something would be haywire.

I left the Beanery late, intending to head home and grab my rest. I had a modest bachelor apartment over on Sixth Avenue, and I was feeling tired enough to welcome hitting the hay, even though it wasn't much after eleven. I nodded to the doorman, who was dozing behind his desk. He never even saw me. I went right up . . . opened the door . . .

'Come in, O'Halloran,' said a coarse voice.

There were two plug-uglies draped across my settee. They were like something out of a Boris Karloff movie, with whiskers and dirty nails. They weren't badly dressed, but they were low types.

They lounged to their feet as I entered; I said: 'What in hell d'you mugs want?'

They leered at me; one came over. 'Siddown.'

'No thanks. I get cramps,' I told him, not wanting to put myself at a disadvantage.

'I says siddown!' he repeated, and handed me a shove on the chest which flattened me into the armchair behind me.

14

He grabbed hold of my mitts, called his buddy over. The other ugly wandered across, fetching a short and thin, but pliant and strong, leather thong from his pocket. I said: 'What . . . ?'

'Lay off the Ancaster Allan story,' the first told me. 'See?'

'Yeah? And who might you be to say about that . . . ?'

The second mug suddenly slashed the thong into my open mouth. It felt as if my tongue had been neatly sheared in two with red-hot knives. I had to scream, loud; the first sap rammed a pillow over my face.

When I was through, he removed the pillow, stuffed my bleeding mouth with a large piece of rag, tight, then watched while his buddy ran a rope round me. I struggled, but I was easy for the tough boys.

Then the first mug said: 'Now give it to the interferin' — !'

2

That beating seemed interminable!

He swiped me viciously about the face, head and neck, not much caring where his blows landed, not much caring if he busted my eyeballs, or knocked half my teeth down my throat.

He was tough — when he was dishing it out. It didn't worry him to think he might be disfiguring a guy for life. I shut my eyes after half a dozen blows, that being the only protection I could afford them, and anyway the blood was running down into them from a rough gash on my forehead. He went on lashing at me until my pan was a mask of searing agony, until the blows fell only dully on my pain-wracked features.

Then his pal stopped him. 'You can lay off now, Leather,' he said, and immediately the blows ceased to fall. I tried to open my peepers to see what was what, but they were gummed tight, and it hurt like hell. I kept them shut. I felt my pockets being searched, felt the copy of the Ancaster Allan story being swiped, then felt the bonds being untied.

The thug who'd supervised the beat-up said: 'Now get this, mister — we ain't playing games here. Either you give the Allan story a miss, or we visit you again. But next time . . . next time, we won't be easy like we were today. Leather — my buddy here — can do a whole lot of things with that thong of his — some of them prove fatal. You get me? That thong's a pretty tight fit round a guy's neck, see what I mean. So if you'll take my tip you'll blow out of town. And say nothing to the cops. But whichever way it goes, you'll skip the story of why Allan blanked himself out.'

Leather grunted: 'Yeah! An' in case you still feel clever, wise guy, here's a reminder!'

I gagged and yelped as the thong bit across my throat; I tipped hazily out of the chair, crashed to the floor, my dukes going up to my throat, my lungs fighting for air. I felt the toe of a heavy boot sashay into my guts, and I started gasping afresh.

When I finally got hold of enough wind to remember what was what, the room was silent.

I tried to open my eyes again; they were bunged-up, and felt hellish sore and tender. My whole face was like a lump of soggy dough after the baker boy'd been kneading it around some. My eyes wouldn't open; I got up, felt my way to the bathroom, turned on the bath taps, let the cold water run. I got the bath nearly full, feeling as if I'd faint at any minute. When I felt the water licking round my fingers where they clutched, the side of the bath, I ducked my turnip and immersed my aching face in the cool water.

It took a whole lot of the pain away instantly, and when I heaved my pan out again I found I could manage to see some by forcing my lids open. I went over to the cabinet mirror, got a look at my face.

Hell! I might have been some guy I'd never seen before. I was puffed, bruised, swollen; blood was caked around my chin and jowls on the day-old stubble of whiskers, and there were gashes in the puffiness of my flesh.

I opened the cabinet and grabbed out some stuff; I poured it over a sponge, then dabbed the whole caboodle on my pan.

That was damn near as painful as Leather's ministrations had been, but I gritted my teeth and kept on soaking. I soaked until I was sure I'd soused every strip of skin, then I got sticking tape and started to build a screen round my mug.

You never saw anything like it!

I saw a movie once, called *The Invisible Man*, and when I looked in the mirror after using that tape, I got a feeling that I could have stepped right in as a double for Claude Rains in that scene where he has his puss blanked right the way out. Anyway, I was hardly showing a square inch of skin from eyebrows to chin, and what was showing was all the colours of the rainbow.

I went into the other room, had a whisky, put on a smoke, and sat down to figure out the next move.

Because if you bozos think I was going

to be licked into a state of yellowness by those two pulled-out streaks of brutality, you're nuts. The whole incident had only made me all the more eager to see what was what, and what was making things tick around that Ancaster Allan story.

One thing was pretty clear to me right there: namely, that I couldn't go to the cops now, because I hadn't got the signed statement to back me up. That led me to another point:

How about Allan's dame, Georgia Dean?

I'd stepped out with Georgia, I'd got the confession from her. I'd spent plenty on her to get it, too; then I'd had her half-drunk before she really spilled the beans. This meant that I would now have to repeat the whole routine. Mind, I wasn't kicking about taking Georgia out — not on your natural. She was one of the sweetest dames I'd seen in many days; but the dough was another question.

You needed dough to take out a high stepper in the chorus of the new musical show which was currently wowing Broadway. Then some. And although I had some dough in hand, I didn't have enough to go doing that sort of thing again.

Besides, even if I steeled myself to parting with a wad, how about my pan? Would any self-respecting chorine be seen out with a guy who looks as though he'd just gotten his pan tangled with the wheels of the rollercoaster at Coney Island? No, she wouldn't.

I was impatient, but I knew there wasn't a thing I could do right then. Except, maybe, if I appealed to her . . . Appealed to her better nature? Did chorines have any of those? Suppose I told her I'd lost my job, had to get another signed statement to get it back. Would that shake her? It was worth the try, anyway.

I had another gander at my pan, groaned dismally and hoped she wouldn't be frightened out of her wits when she saw me, slung on hat and coat, and went out.

I was kind of embarrassed, and I had cause to be. I don't know if you ever noticed it, but let a guy who's bandaged or plastered up all over his pan walk abroad where there's people, and the very first thing that happens is that he's what the novelists call the 'cynosure of all eyes'.

I was that all right. It began with the old lady I passed on the steps. She almost dropped her bag, and moved hurriedly over to the opposite side as if I had an infectious disease. I grunted, pulled a face at her with the bit I had left, and had the pleasure of hearing her give a nervous gasp and shoot like all hell up the steps and into the building.

Next thing I know I'm walking along, hat pulled low, and a big beefy Irish cop walking behind me suspiciously.

He caught me up on the corner, gave me the eye, then said:

'Are you in throuble, me boy?'

'No, I ain't in any throuble,' I mimicked, getting mad. 'Can't a guy walk out with a piece of plaster on his pan now without you lugs sifting in?'

He grunted, said: 'You look as if you'd had grief.'

'I have — got my face caught in the bedroom door. That's what comes of trying to get in someplace you ain't wanted. Good night, pal.'

I left him staring after me and scratching his head. But even then I wasn't free.

Folks kept turning and staring, passing remarks to each other. I passed a cinema queue, heard them say:

'Oh, *look*!'

'That *poor* man . . . '

'What do you suppose . . . ?'

'Jeepers, *what* a face!'

The Irish in me boiled right over; I grabbed off my hat, stood in front of them, rapped: 'Sure, get yourselves a good look while you can, folks! Help yourselves, it's for free. Funny, ain't it?'

Then — was I mad! A dear old lady suddenly wipes a tear from the corner of her eyes as she is passing, and drops a nickel in my hat!

I stood staring at it for a minute, while the queue rubbered at me. Then I let go of an ungentlemanly cuss word, slung the nickel into the gutter, rammed my lid on, and walked on.

Larry O'Halloran, I told myself, you ask for it, and when you get it you don't like it.

I didn't boil up again; I kept going, ignoring people who stared, and finally got as far as the theatre where Georgia

Dean was making her appearance as a pair of legs, third from right, front row.

I went along to the stage entrance, elbowed my way through a bunch of johnnies, walked inside.

The door keeper yelled: 'Hey, where you going, mister?'

I turned round, said: 'Don't be funny, Joe. Press.'

' 'Press', my neck,' he yapped, and I'd have taken him at his word only he was inside his little booth and I couldn't get at him. 'You ain't any pressman *I* know.'

'Get wise, Joe,' I snorted. 'The name's O'Halloran . . . '

'Larry?' He gawked. '*You're* Larry O'Halloran?' He peers over his glasses at my plastered face, then says: 'Say, you *do* look like Mr. O'Halloran a bit at that! What you been doing to yourself?' He cackled.

'If you think I've done this to *myself* you're crazy,' I snap.

I walk on, and he calls after me: 'Sorry, I didn't recognise you. But you can't blame me, can you?'

I didn't answer that. I went to the side of the stage, acquainted the stage manager with my identity, and stood and watched.

Georgia was on stage, doing a Mexican number with the rest of the girls. The stage manager followed my gaze, said: 'Interested in Miss Dean, Larry?'

'What if I am?' I muttered.

'Don't get excited, don't get excited. I know how it is — you reporters . . . ' and he winked blandly at nothing in particular.

'What about us reporters?' I growled.

'Har, har,' he told me. 'Har, har, har. You know. Har, har!'

'You got whooping cough — better get it seen to.'

He ignored that crack about his style of laughing. Said: 'She stands out from the rest, doesn't she?'

I admitted she did.

'She's set for a great career — Ancaster Allan was going to put her into his next play as leading lady. Pity he died. For her.'

'Sure; but she isn't cut out for the dramatic stage. She's essentially musical comedy, anyone can see that.'

'Sure. Maybe you didn't know she's

been picked for the lead in the next show here?'

'No, I didn't know that. But I wish her plenty of luck.'

'She'll need it. The audiences here are tough babies when it comes to leading ladies from Brooklyn, which is where she's from. But she'll get by . . . on those legs.'

'With the male section at least.' I grinned.

'That's what counts.'

The number finished, and I turned and walked upstairs to her dressing room. The four chorines who shared it came tumbling in, and in a hurry to make their change. Before I had a chance to make myself known, they were taking things off, but fast.

I said: 'Hey, hey! Not in front of the children, *please*!'

They all spun round. Someone said: 'A man . . . *a man*!' and then one hell of a shriek went up and they grabbed for dressing gowns and things.

I said: 'Not a man, kids — a reporter.'

The dressing gowns were downed; Georgia said: 'That's different. You here for an interview? And what happened to your face?'

'That cat trod on me, to your second,' I told her. 'And to your first, I'm here for an interview with *you*.'

'Which paper are you from?'

'*Recorder*,' I said briefly, deciding it would be wiser not to say I'd been fired.

'*Recorder*? Do you know someone called O'Halloran?' she asked.

I said: 'But sure I do. A nice guy.'

'He is, isn't he?' she said, reflectively. 'I think so too.'

I blushed some under by bands of plaster. I hadn't known I'd made any impression as big as that on her. I said: 'Yep, I can say safely that O'Halloran's my best friend. A swell feller.'

She nodded, sliding into a brief pair of trunks for her next number. The other girls had now lost interest since I wasn't there to give them any publicity. They were not noticing us. I said:

'I'd like to see you after the show for a private talk.'

She shook her head. 'I can't. I'm rather busy. But I'll answer any questions you want to ask right here. Go ahead.'

'No can do. Make it after the show?'

'Sorry, no. If your paper want any private interviews like that, tell your editor to send O'Halloran.'

'You don't get it,' I told her. '*I am O'Halloran!*'

'You *are* . . . you're *not!*'

She staggered a bit, disbelief in her eyes.

'It's a fact. I had trouble. See, here's my Press card. I was fired from the *Recorder* today, and you can help me get another job. Do that and I'll plug you any time I get a chance. That's why I want to see you tonight, baby. Can do?'

She nodded dumbly. 'Yes, Larry — but — what happened?'

'I'll tell you: there was a guy walking along Fifth today. I hadn't ever done him any harm. Hadn't spoken a wrong word to him. In fact, I didn't even know him. On the other hand it might have been a dog! Whichever it was was hungry . . . '

'But — what's *that* to do with it?' she asked, amazed.

'I'm getting to that. Have a bit of

patience. He, or it, was hungry and eating . . . of all things, a banana! Two hours or maybe more, or less, later, *I* had to walk along that very same route . . . get it?'

'I get one thing: you're lying. You didn't get that face by slipping on any banana skins, and you know it as well as I do. How did it happen, Larry?'

Somebody yelled: 'Onstage for the Woodland number.'

'You'd better go now,' I told her. 'Or you'll miss your cue.'

'Oh, yes.' She flew towards the door.

I bawled: 'Hey! I'll wait in the passage, and . . . '

'And what?'

'Hadn't you better put your costume on, or do you appear in stage trunks and bra?'

★   ★   ★

She picked me up at the end of the show, and we walked out.

I said, as we, left the theatre: 'Georgia, you've been holding out on me. You know more about the Allan affair than you've said. I want you to make a clean breast with me . . . '

She frowned, looking thoughtful, and a touch worried.

'If I do, you won't let any harm come to me, Larry?'

'Cross the place where my heart ought to be,' I vowed.

She nodded: 'Come up to my place — I'll give you a light.'

'Then you do know more — you know who was doing the blackmailing, maybe?'

'Not that; but I can tell you what it was Ancaster wanted kept quiet. So quiet that he was willing to hand over thousands of dollars to have it kept that way. And I can show you one or two of the blackmail notes. I — I found them in some love letters I'd sent to him. In a bundle — they must have got mixed up.'

'That's just swell,' I smiled. 'You're a good kid, Georgia.'

And then I saw the car: it was sneaking along, engine purring, rolling towards us up the side street which led to Broadway! I saw more than that — I saw the muzzle of a sub (and I don't mean a sub-editor!)

peeking through the rear window. And as it picked up pace I flung Georgia flat and followed her. I yelled: '*Keep low!*'

The next thing the bewildered girl was clambering to her feet saying: 'Larry — have you gone mad?'

3

There wasn't a thing I could do; she hadn't seen the car coming along, she didn't know the danger there was in the back of that closed sedan.

She was saying: 'What are you playing at, Larry?' and I was coming to my feet again to pull her down, when the harsh rattle of the sub bit holes in the silence, and lead spewed out against the wall back of me.

It didn't all hit the wall though!

The bozos in the sedan must have seen I was flat, and maybe they couldn't grab a fair aim at me lying there — maybe they didn't want to. Whichever way it was the gunman took his aim high, and the bullets splattered into her, well above the chest-line.

Then the car was gone and she was still standing there as if she'd been paralysed; standing swaying slightly, not making any sound at all.

I was up to my knees when she toppled over like a felled tree, and came cannoning down on top of me. I felt the warm, sticky blood; I squirmed from under, stared into her glazed eyes. She was as dead as they ever come. Her neckline and shoulders were almost severed from her torso.

What a hell of a waste of beauty, I thought, and I was too numbed to realise properly that she was dead, and there wasn't any bringing her back, and maybe it was all my fault for being such a long-nosed skunk.

All this happened in seconds; then, I heard a nightstick hammering the sidewalk farther along, and I spotted the whole convoy of ordinary people, attracted from the main stem by the death rattle of the submachine gun, swarming like a horde of locusts towards the scene of the tragedy.

They do swarm that way; ghouls, the presence of physical pain, even death, drawing them like a magnet draws iron filings. They stand and gape, and gawk, and pore over the pools of blood around the point, and they wait for the ambulance and watch the corpse being lifted into it, watch it screech away, and if the unlucky hombre isn't already dead they take wagers on his chances of survival.

Then they go home and tell the folks all about what they saw, and in the end none of them can handle their dinners or suppers. So they take some stomach powder to settle them, and the following day they've clear forgotten all about it, and they're prowling about, always alert for fresh accidents.

Maybe you've heard about fire-chasers? Those guys who always tail hooks and ladders in their cars to the scene of the fire? Yeah, it's a great American pastime. And so is ambulance chasing! Only that's even worse in my opinion, if it counts for anything, which it doesn't — not any more.

I had reached my feet and was standing upright by the time the first vultures arrived on the scene. But in next to no time at all the crowd was as thick as a bunch of Brooklyn boys waiting to get in to see the Dodgers play ball. Where they all sprung from in an alley that had been deserted minutes before I don't know, and never hope to guess. But there they were. And right among them was the beefy Irish cop I'd spoken to on the way. I don't know why I made that sudden decision to stay out of the whole shemozzle. But I did know I couldn't help track down the men in that sedan, nor the car itself, because I hadn't seen a thing except that sub poking from the window. And I did know I was in for a lot of grief if I got tangled with police lines at this point. What is more to the point, however, when I had seen Georgia crash over like she had, all shot up, I had made a vow to myself which was still as good as when it had impulsively flashed over my mind. A vow to get the thugs who had done it, and see them fry for their sins, or die doing it.

And I was wise enough to know that if the cops ventured into the game on the scanty evidence I could supply, they might gum up the entire works.

At that point I became aware of the cop saying: 'Hmm. Seems like there wasn't anybody with her, bedad. Did any of yez see anyone here, did yez?'

'Yez' shook their heads. He said: 'Who was the first on the scene?'

Nobody seemed able to answer that; they'd come up in a kind of rush in the darkness, and they hadn't realised I'd been in on it as well as the girl. To them I was one of themselves, a gaping, gawking ghoul, with the smell of fresh blood in my nostrils, and the strange, warped excitement which disaster and misery gave to them, in my veins!

The cop started to sort out the crowd, trying to find witnesses. It wasn't hard to duck aside and elbow my way out. More and more people were surging down the alleyway, until it was packed from top to end. I jostled right through without minding how many sets of ribs I bust, and my plastered face went unnoticed in the excitement of knowing someone had been bumped off so close to Broadway.

I hit the main stem; flagged a passing cab. I murmured: 'Cranforth Apartment Buildings, buddy, and pedal your scooter.'

He pedalled it; we cut neatly through the traffic, and in next to no time I was in my rooms, sagged out in the chair, bracing up my spirits with a peg of brandy. I felt as miserable as hell!

But I gradually got hold of myself again and started to think. If I was tracking down the killers, I'd have to start someplace. I needed a lead — I wasn't going to get anywhere sitting on my fanny, percolating brandy down my throat, and thinking what a sweet lovely Georgia used to be. No, sir. I had to start. And lurking round the back of what passes for my mind was a lead that seemed to promise some, if not much, fruit.

Georgia had told me she had a couple or so of the notes which the blackmailer had sent along to Allan. Obviously those notes were up in her apartment. Equally obviously, the blackmailer couldn't know they were in her possession — so what?

So I had to get them, and right now, before the busies stepped in and started mussing her place up trying to find a clue to why she'd been gunned down. I got up again, tilted my hat, phoned a taxi, and headed out.

The cab met me at the corner, and I told him to drop me at a point about a hundred yards from Georgia's apartment. I paid him off, watched him streak away. Then I walked quickly down the street and in at the doors of the Layforth building.

I operated the automatic elevator; there was no one to see me come or go; the Layforth sported a janitor, but he was in back most probably, making merry with coffee and cakes.

I'd been in before, so I knew just where to get off. I got off at the third, found her outer suite door.

It was locked, and I'd expected that. But I remembered the topography of the joint, and went along to the end corridor window. I got through this on to the stone balcony, which was really just a ledge, no more than three inches wide. I caught hold of the grooved stones just over my head, worked my way along. I was counting on the fact that, offstage, Georgia had been a fresh air fiend, and I wasn't let down. The window of her place was open about two foot. A push, and it was wide enough for me to step in with a sigh of relief.

I clicked the light switch by the door,

glanced round. There was no time for caution; in a few seconds, maybe the cops would have traced her identity, found her address, and would be up. I had to be gone by then or I'd be headed for trouble.

Where would a dame like Georgia have stacked letters? Writing desk? No, that was too obvious. I hadn't any delusions that she'd have some letters which wouldn't show her up too well if seen by anyone. She'd probably have a fairly safe hidey-hole for her used mail.

I found it the second try, in an old shoe box in the bottom of the wardrobe, I emptied the mail out on the table, started skimming through the envelopes. Only two bore a typed address, and the name of Ancaster Allan. I grabbed those two and stuffed them in my pockets. And then . . . I heard the sound of many large feet hawking along towards the door!

The cops!

I waited, holding my wind; if I headed out of the bedroom and they walked right in, they'd get me for sure. I daredn't chance it.

Then I heard: 'Locked — go find the

janitor, Brusset; and get him to bring his keyring up here. Hurry it up.'

I breathed again, tiptoed out across the room, clipped the light-switch off. I heard the cop outside say: 'What was that? That clicking noise?'

I didn't wait for the answer if he got one. I beat it out on the ledge again, glad even to get back to that perilous trip, rather than face a bunch of inquiring bulls of a jaundiced frame of mind. I hit the passage window and peered . . .

I was in time to see the janitor roll along, fit his key, and open up. They all poured in, janitor as well, leaving the passage empty. I got a leg over the sill, then suddenly heard the elevator doors opening. I looked up . . .

A reporter from my own rag, the *Recorder*, was coming out of the elevator. When he saw me his face opened some in the region of his mouth. He stopped and stared.

I came in fast, all the way, started along towards him. He took a couple of uncertain steps backwards, before I called, softly:

'Jimmy — Jimmy Edwards — it's me, O'Halloran.'

His pan was a perfect blank as he stared. He said: 'Larry — what the printer's devil have you been up to now?'

'It's all right, Jimmy. Forget you saw me — don't say a thing to the cops about me being here. I've got reasons for not wanting them to know.'

'But what — why?'

'I'm taking it for granted that you know what's happened to Georgia Dean,' I told him, and he nodded.

'That's why I'm here, covering the story.'

'Then you can save yourself the trouble, because I'm telling you that if you find out anything above bare details, they won't run the story. It bears on the Ancaster Allan case. They won't print it.'

He looked curious. 'That's how you lost *your* job, isn't it?'

'Yeah, that's it.'

'And you're still tangling in the case?'

'I am. That's the reason I came up here.'

He shook his head sadly, said: 'Why

don't you get some sense, Larry? Where will you get, running after your own tail? You know the whole business is poison for the press.'

'Why?' I shot out.

He shrugged. 'How should I know why? I just know it is. Look what happened to you — look at the orders we've had.'

'Sure, I'm looking. And if that's the kind of newsman you want to be, you're welcome, Jimmy. I'm different. There's something smelly behind all this, and I'm finding out what. When I do I'll expose the whole damn newspaper racket for concealing facts. When I do I'll show the people of America what their so-called free press really is. When I do . . . '

'Quit idealising,' he told me, grinning. 'You always did fly off the handle too easy.'

I snorted. 'Okay, I'm idealising. So what? At least I'm playing for what's right, and I'm going to get it.'

'You're going to *get it* all right,' he grunted. 'But what you get isn't going to be what you want. You can't buck up against whoever causes these stories to be suppressed. Hell, they must have the devil of a lot of pull. Besides . . . how you going to fix it now? You're off the *Recorder*, no other rag'll have you, they tell me. How can you print any exposures when you don't work anymore? Tell me that?'

For the minute he had me; and I felt one awful sap, because he was absolutely right. How was I going to do anything about the other papers when I didn't work for any of them? When they were all in league against me?

Then I got it. I said, triumphantly: 'It's easy, Jimmy. I'm starting my own sheet!'

He had to hang on to the elevator door for support. He jumped. Said: 'You're — you're *what*?'

'My own sheet,' I told him, nonchalantly. 'How'd you like that?'

'You're kidding. You're haywire. You couldn't.'

'No? And why couldn't I? Sure I could if I want to.'

'But the competition — you're up against . . . '

'I know — up against a bunch of

blasted hypocrites who're supposed to dish out news for the general public, but who keep back anything they don't want printed. Oh, I know it isn't the reporters' fault, it isn't the editors' fault, and it isn't anybody's fault who works on the paper. But *someone's* at back of it. And when my own rag's running, nobody'll dictate to me what I put in and what I don't. My policy'll be to print whatever happens to be the news. And I'll use this as my first story!'

He was still opening and shutting his mouth, as if he couldn't get used to anyone having the nerve to buck up against the big paper combines. He said, at last: 'You on the level . . . ?'

'Why, sure.'

'What'll you call your sheet?'

I thought quickly. I said: 'I'll call it the *Bombshell*. That's what it'll *be*!'

He suddenly began to grin. 'You can't do it, Larry. You know it.'

'Why not?'

'You know damned well why not. In the first place you need one hell of a lot of dough to get started. Comic features, magazine supplement, features, news section, photogravure section, and all the rest of it. Dozens of pages — and what could you retail it at? I'll tell you. Ten cents a copy, maybe, if anyone would buy it; would that cover production cost? Not on your life!

'You've got to rely on advertising for making the paper pay. And tell me where you're going to grab a million bucks' worth of advertising contracts, and get advance payment to cover your first copy? Tell me that?'

'I'll tell you something else,' I said, getting het up. 'Why do today's papers have to offer comics, magazine supplements, photogravure work, features, stories, Winchell, murder and sex? I'll tell you: because there isn't any beef in them! That's why. That's why they run to sixty and more pages. Because the public wouldn't pay a cent to read the news they print. It doesn't count. Eighty per cent of the public aren't interested in seeing a pic of a famous society dame showing what passes for legs on Park Avenue. They get the same news in every paper . . . but if there was a sheet which was different — which printed items none of the other rags dared to print, exposed anything that wasn't in the public interest — *then* what?'

'You'd still flop.'

'You're wrong. Everybody'd buy it. That's why they'll buy my sheet. Exclusives. I'm telling you here and now it'll only run to *two pages*! That's all. But every sentence'll be packed with sensation. They won't get any advertisement, but they'll pay ten cents for it just like the other sixty-page efforts. They'll pay because if they don't they'll be out of it. Everyone else will have a copy. It'll work. It *has* to work. The first special will wow them.'

He still shook his head.

'You see — you won't get away with it. Even if they did buy, you wouldn't last hours. The big combines'd crush you!'

'I said I'm going to publish it, and I am. You watch out for the first edition of the *Manhattan Bombshell*!'

And I took the elevator down; what I had said half in bluff at first had now got a grip of me. My own sheet! Print what I liked when I liked! I was fired with resolution, heedless of any trouble in store. There'd be plenty of that — but I'd run the *Manhattan Bombshell* or bust myself trying!

4

I slept on it that night.

In the morning, when I took a look in my shave mirror, my pan had considerably improved. It was still bulbous-looking, and the cuts made thin lines of dried blood; but after I'd got the plaster off, and washed and shaved — tentatively — I felt like a new man, and admitted that my mother would, maybe, have known me now after all.

I was still full of the idea; it was getting a grip on me, and a night's sleep hadn't done anything to dim the brightness of my vision — except that I realised the difficulties more fully.

But I was determined to overcome any trouble which lay in the way of realising my ambitions. *Manhattan Bombshell*, I swore to myself, would be off the press within the month — maybe much sooner if it could be fixed!

My first stop that morning was at my

bank; I checked on my account. Four thousand dollars.

'Okay, I'll take it all,' I told the manager.

'All, Mr. O'Halloran? But — it's taken you years . . . '

'I know it. But maybe within the month I'll have treble that amount to pay in. Maybe not. Just the same, I'll take it all, and no questions!'

'Well, just as you say, Mr. O'Halloran.'

When I went out my billfold was loaded with hundred-dollar bills. I was feeling pretty high, and went along to my next stop.

This was an agency office downtown. The fat, chiselling runt who ran it was a friend of mine — don't blame me, when you're a newsman you pick up some funny friends — and now, for the first time, I figured he might come in useful.

'A modest office, Mr. O'H.?' he said, rubbing his hands. 'Yes, we can do that for you. There's a vacancy in the Excelsior block, fifth floor: four outer, one inner office. Two-fifty a week.'

'If you mean two-fifty cents, okay,' I

said shortly. 'If you mean bucks, wash it out. I'm O'Halloran, not Rockefeller. Come down some, Meadle.'

He grunted, said: 'That's cheap, O'H. What did you want to pay?'

'I want to pay about two bucks a week, but I expect I'll have to pay more. Anyway, I'll go to fifty per week, not a cent over.'

He didn't look any too pleased, but he scrabbled through files and forms. At last he looked at me.

'One here at forty-five,' he told me. 'One outer, one inner. Inter-office communication, elevator service . . . '

'That'll suit,' I said quickly.

'*Fortieth* floor,' he leered.

'Okay.'

'But Mr. O'H., you don't want to walk up all those stairs.'

'You said there was an elevator service?'

'I know — there is. When it's running. But the building's old as buildings go, and the district isn't very classy. The elevator's as old as the building, and often it goes wrong. Why not take some place a little higher in price — say, about a hundred?'

'No dice. I'll take what you offered.'

'But the *stairs* . . . ?'

'I *like* stairs!' I glared at him, and he shut up.

I paid a deposit on the key, said: 'If it isn't worth forty-five, I'll be back to readjust things.'

'You'll find it all right. I wouldn't cheat a friend of mine.'

'Are you kidding? You'd cheat your own grandmother, if you could.'

He smirked fatly. 'Why d'you want an office in such a hurry, O'H.?' he said. 'I thought you worked for the *Recorder*?'

'Not any longer. The chief got tired of my face. I'm starting my own sheet, Meadle.'

'You're what?' His eyes popped at me.

'My own sheet,' I told him, then explained about everything.

At length he nodded, and his brow was corrugated in thought. Then he snapped open a desk drawer and filched out a wad. He peeled off ten hundred-dollar bills, threw them over.

I said: 'Hey? What gives?'

'I'm coming in,' he chuckled. 'I think

you've got something, and I guess it'll boom. I'm in for a thousand. You can make me a receipt out before you go.'

'There's one thing,' I snapped. 'I'm anxious to take your chips, but get this: I keep the controlling percentage of this paper. I'm running it the way I want. Nobody but me gets a say in the editorial policy. See? There'll be no board of directors, and there'll be no committee meetings. I'm the big cheese, and I'm staying that way. Now, if you don't like that, grab your change and get out while you can.'

He waved his hand. He said: 'The sheet'll pay off — I'm sure of that. If I wasn't I wouldn't be coming in with you, take my word for it. Keep the dough. I'm agreeable to you being the boss.'

I made him a receipt out; if a shrewd old goat like J.F. Meadle was willing to throw good money into a harebrained enterprise like I'd outlined, there must be something in it from his point of view. Because Meadle wouldn't spend a cent unless he was sure he'd get back at least a nickel!

I left for my new office, considerably elated.

Five Gs in hand. Surely enough to rush out the first edition of my *Bombshell*? It didn't have to be a big circulation for the start. A modest fifty thousand would do all right. It would pass from hand to hand, and the dough it brought in would pay for the second week's edition to be doubled in quantity. Later, I could make it a daily, maybe.

Things sure looked bright. I was heading somewhere now, and I was going on . . .

I was heading for the office, to be more exact. It was in a down-at-heel district, in what I always called 'Sub-Manhattan', but it didn't matter a lot where I started.

I was sandwiched in between theatrical agents of low repute, safe agencies, town offices for small factories out of town, and a hundred other varied forms of making dough. I didn't give a damn about that either. The paper was the thing, and I could have worked on that first edition in a slit trench! And maybe I'd have to before I was through!

The office itself was in a hellish state. Old papers, dust, and broken-down chairs lay scattered about the room. In the outer office, at the reception desk, there was a typewriter which appeared to have been well and truly lambasted with a fourteen pound hammer. Odd letters lay about in the inner office, and I picked one up with a view to getting a line on the previous tenants. It was dated some months before, and read:

Ajax Song Writing Agency.
Dear Sirs,
I submitted my song, 'Love is Like a Pretty Flower' to you, one year ago, and later forwarded the hundred dollars' expense of marketing you requested. Since that time I have received a payment of seventy-five cents royalties, six copies of sheet music, and nothing more. Would you kindly forward outstanding royalties owing to me to the above address, as I am badly in need of money.
Faithfully,
Gershwin Jackson

The address mentioned was in Kansas!

I had to grin; couldn't help it. Obviously the Ajax people had been setting a sucker trap, and had caught some fine fish. There were other letters about, all similar in content. Something must have gone wrong with the works, and this was the result. The agency had folded its tents like the Arabs and as silently gone away!

One of them, maybe a humorist, had scrawled on the table: 'Back in fifty years!'

I picked up another letter, on top of the heap, and dated only two months ago. It read:

> *Dear Sirs,*
>
> *Many thanks for your letter telling me that orders for my song 'Wagon Wheel Boogie' are pouring in. I send the additional three hundred dollars you ask for herewith. Don't send the royalties next month, as I am coming to New York to take up residence, when I hope to have the pleasure of writing many more songs for you.*
>
> *Yours sincerely,*
> *Valerie Romain.*

Easy to see what had happened there, for instance. The rats had told the dame what a swell song she'd written, had said it was on production, had been plugged on the radio, maybe, and orders were rolling in. But the terms of the contract would specify that she paid for publication of the sheet music, and took about a third or a half share in profits.

Naturally she'd never see her dough again; maybe that was why they'd skipped town, to dodge her visit.

And that one came from Greenville, S. Carolina.

I wondered what the she was like, and visualised some dried-up old dame; then I took another look at the song title, 'Wagon Wheel Boogie', and forgot about old dames. No old frail could have turned out anything with a title like that; or I didn't think so.

I surveyed the office, then I picked up the phone, which was on again. I said into it: 'Central one-double-o, four-double-five, o.'

I got through to a domestic agency, said: 'Could you let me have a couple of office cleaners right now?'

They could. They did. The two old ladies arrived within twenty minutes, and started making merry with the debris.

I was still on the phone, to the Acme Typewriter Company now. I ordered two of their newest models for the office. I had my own portable, which would help out. Then I contacted the office filters who'd supplied the equipment for the *Recorder*. I put in an order for a roll-top, two plain, a couple of armchairs, and four round-back office chairs. Carpet and filing cabinets completed my order there. The windows already had shades up. The chars had finished their ministrations by that time, and I paid them off and stood in the middle of a spotless office, waiting for the furniture to arrive. The typewriters came and were set on the floor, there being nowhere else for them. Then there was another knock at the door, and I opened it . . .

A stunning girl stood there. She had golden hair, attractively done; nice red lips, and eyes which were fascinating.

I said: 'Come into my parlour . . . '

She was in; she looked round in some surprise. She said: 'You don't know me . . .'

'We can remedy that.'

She blushed a bit. She said: 'I wrote a song for you . . . my name is Romain — Valerie Romain. I've called to see if I can pick up my royalties — the truth is, I'm a little short of ready money. The three hundred I sent you, and my fare, cleaned me out.'

There was a faint trace of Southern accent in her soft voice; not much, just a husky broadness which served to make it warm and genuine.

'Valerie Romain? Why, sure. I've just been reading through one of your letters. How do you do, Miss Romain?'

'I'm very well, thank you. You're . . . ?'

'My name's O'Halloran. And I'm the new tenant here.'

'New — new tenant?'

'Yes, I'm afraid so.'

'But — my royalties — the Ajax Company . . . ?'

'Have flown the coop, or vamoosed the ranch house.'

Her face looked pretty startled, and a bit desperate. 'They can't have — they owe me money . . . I . . . how . . . ?'

'Don't mind me being blunt, Miss Romain,' I told her, regretfully.'But I'm afraid you've been taken for a sucker. Like a whole lot of other people. The Ajax agency was a fraud.'

'Oh, no! Mr. O'Halloran . . . where are they?'

'That, nobody knows. It's a time-worn game, and it's surprising the number of folks who still fall for it. Extortion without any violence, and without too much risk.'

'But . . . look here, they *did* publish my song. See, I have a copy or two they sent to me.'

She produced a sheet of music, with a lurid cover bearing the words *WAGON WHEEL BOOGIE by Valerie Romain*, from her handbag. I took it and grinned. I said: 'Sure, they publish about six sheets of this, send it along to their clients, and then sit back. Far as they're concerned, that's the end of the matter.'

'The police . . . ?'

'Can't do anything until they overstep themselves, as they did when they told you orders were rolling in. Probably they knew you'd make trouble for them with the letters they'd sent, and skipped town. They won't be traceable; I'm afraid it wouldn't do you any good to appeal to the cops.'

She glanced about helplessly: 'But that was all the money I had . . . does it mean my songs are no good?'

'I can't judge about that,' I told her. 'They may or may not be. The Ajax Agency aren't concerned about merit. They just want the dough.'

'Then I can still sell this song elsewhere?'

'No. No publisher would accept it if you've got a contract with the Ajax people.'

'Why?'

'For the simple reason that if it made a hit, the Ajax gang would step in and sue for breach of contract.'

'But if they're crooked . . . '

'There's lawyers as crooked as they are, and there'd be some legal angle to put them in the right if the case was worth fighting out. No decent publisher would override another contract, no matter what the Ajax folk are. Besides, have you any idea how many guys and dames are hawking songs round New York daily? I won't tell you, it might sour your whole outlook. But it's plenty.'

'Oh, dear. What on earth am I going to do? I — I threw in my job in Greenville, and . . . '

I looked her up and down and down and up, and then sideways. She shifted a little, uncomfortably. I said: 'What did you do in your home town?'

'I was a secretary to a local businessman.'

'New York's a wicked city for girls from the South — especially beautiful girls. If I were you . . . '

'Don't say it. I won't.'

'Won't what? How'd you know what I meant to say?'

'I've seen plenty of movies. I know they always tell girls like myself to go back home, and settle down with the nice young boy from the local drugstore. And you needn't advise me *that* way. I stay.'

'I wasn't going to advise you that way,'

I told her. 'I was going to tell you that if I were you, I'd be careful what kind of man I worked for. Pick carefully — someone, for instance, like me.'

'Like — *you*?' she said in some surprise.

I nodded. 'Sure. Now, I'm just starting in business. I need a girl as reception-desk-clerk-cum-typist-cum- . . . a lot of other things.'

'A lot of — *other* things?'

'Purely business things. I'm starting a newssheet . . . I . . . '

'You're offering *me* a job?' she gasped. 'I know nothing about newspaper work.'

'That's what I mean. This sheet is going to be different. All recognised procedure and precedent is going to the wall. It won't pay a lot, but it'll be darned interesting. I'll take you on a three-week trial at twenty dollars a week, if you're interested. When the rag gets on its feet, the pay'll go up accordingly. How about it?'

My enthusiasm infected her; I'd snapped her into it. She hesitated one or two seconds, then said: 'If *you're* willing to risk it, why should *I* refuse? Thank you, Mr. O'Halloran, I'm your woman!'

5

I headed down to the office early the following morning. If I was going to get *Manhattan Bombshell* on the stands within the next couple of weeks, there was plenty to do.

Valerie was at the reception desk, and she gave me a big smile when I came in. I said: 'Hello, gorgeous. Like the new furniture?'

'It's fine,' she told me seriously, dabbing at the keys of her typewriter. 'But — will these two offices be enough to do all the work in?'

'Plenty. I'll do most of it myself. I'll need just one hound to round up local data. I'll shove out an ad for a routine man today.'

But I didn't need to shove any ad out. I got a visit from Jimmy Edwards off the *Recorder* — you remember, the guy who spotted me sneaking round Georgia's apartment the other night — and he was feeling cooperative. He came right to the point.

'Hear you're getting your tabloid under way?'

'S'right.'

'You'll need a staff man, won't you? Take on routine work?'

I nodded, wondering what he was leading up to. He went on:

'I'm okay as far as that goes.'

'You offering your services?' I exploded.

He grunted, said: 'That's about the size of it. I'm going to throw in with the *Recorder* and give you my extraordinary talent for what it's worth.'

'It's about thirty bucks a week only, to me,' I told him.

I'd expected him to jib at that, because as a junior on the *Recorder* he was drawing down fifty. But he didn't jib. He said:

'I play ball.'

'You mean you'll work for thirty bucks a week for me?'

'Not for you — for your idea. I've been thinking over what you said. This town needs a rag like the *Bombshell*. I'd like to help someway. You're salting away trouble, O'Halloran — plenty of it. But I'm willing to take all the trouble we can get and work for the same thing you're working for — a freer press, and a cleaner city, and all that highfalutin stuff you spouted last night. You got me convinced.'

I shook his hand. 'I guess that speech I handed you did make an impression on that lump of bone you call a head, eh, Jimmy? Okay, you work for me — as soon as you're through on the *Recorder*.'

'I *am* through. I blew out this morning . . . '

'But, why?'

'You remember what you said about the Allan case? Well, I ran some copy out on that line, putting it to the public to decide whether the shooting of Georgia Dean had anything to do with the suicide of Allan. I hinted at blackmail . . . '

'And . . . ?'

'I got a bawling-out from the chief, because I hadn't done as I was told and forgotten the Allan case. What you said last night was still under my hair, so I simply told him where he left the trolley, and walked out. That's how I came to find you here.'

'Nice work. You're the boy I've been

wanting. You know the routine you follow at the *Recorder* — you follow the same here, except if you get any hot leads we play them for all we're worth. Now you can take over while I head out and see to one or two little things.'

I left him arranging the spare desk to his liking; I was lucky to grab off an experienced boy like Jimmy Edwards for thirty.

I went across town to see Hammerton-Williams, head of the biggest distribution agency in the city. I found him in, and tackled him in his office. I came right out with it:

'I'm running a paper called the *Manhattan Bombshell*. I'd like you to take over distribution for me.'

He shook his head, firmly: 'Sorry. Can't do that, Larry.'

'Why not?' I demanded aggressively. 'If you get the usual percentage, why can't you?'

'I don't handle papers, you know that. They go from press to stall, mostly.'

'You don't get it — mine'll be a weekly, more of a tabloid. The news I print will hold good after the other sheets are being used to wrap last week's laundry up in. You can handle it until it achieves daily status, then I'll pay you a handsome bonus. Can do?'

'Still sorry, Larry. Can't take it on.'

I was getting excited about it. I bawled: 'For the love of Mike, why can't you?'

'You want me to be frank with you?'

'Sure, go ahead.'

'I will. I respect my trade connections far too much.'

'But what's that to do with it? You handle magazines and small weeklies. My rag won't crash *their* territory.'

'It isn't that either. I handle a whole lot of out of town and overseas editions of the daily papers. And — well, I'll give it you straight, Larry: I've already heard of your plan to start a paper. And I've been requested by several newspaper owners not to take your paper in hand for distribution. If I do, they let me know that they'd hand over their business to someone else. I couldn't stand that loss. No, I can't do a thing for you. Sorry.'

I was so burned up I didn't dare speak. It was going to be tougher even than I thought, now. But I wasn't anywhere near beat. I hiked round to Sidney Glassmer, a small-time distributor, who was game to handle anything from carnival hats to babies' rattles, and who ran a good line of cheap fictional books at twenty-five cents. I found him more receptive.

'Sure, I'll handle your paper, Larry,' he told me. 'I'll get my salesmen out boosting it tomorrow, and I'll shove it on my next order list. I don't figure you'll do a lot of trade charging ten cents for two pages, but maybe I'm wrong.'

'I think you will be, Sid, and, thanks.'

I spent the remainder of the day touring round the newsagents I knew, taking in the big stalls at the stations, and the stalls near the ferry, and the whole of the bigger combines. I solicited a few useful orders; when they found it was returnable if unsold, they didn't mind taking the chance.

Then I went back to the office: it was getting on for five, and Valerie was putting on a new face to beat it home, or to wherever she hung out. She looked cuter than ever, and I said: 'How about you and me going stepping tonight?'

'There wasn't anything about letting you date me in our arrangements,' she told me gravely. 'I don't know — I've heard all newsmen are wolves.'

'So we are — but nice wolves. We aren't vicious, Val.'

She smiled. 'All right, Larry. I'll chance it this once. Where'll we meet?'

'The clock at Grand Central will do. We can get wherever we want to go from there.'

I watched her hip movement as she went out, then I slammed through into the inner office. There was a note lying on the desk. It was from Jimmy.

Gone out to cover a Bronx murder. There's a letter in the right-hand drawer of your desk. Jimmy.

I opened my desk drawer and took out a thin envelope of a common type. I slit it along with my thumb, noticing the postmark was a New York one. I extracted the sheet of paper inside. Typewritten. Brief. And murderous.

Be warned before you go too far, O'Halloran. Stop your foolish scheme to start a newspaper exposure. You are watched continually . . . The RAVEN!

★   ★   ★

I picked up Valerie sharp at six-thirty as arranged, and at her suggestion we went to a quiet chop suey parlour for dinner. Over the coffee I showed her the note, said:

'It may or may not be a joke. Personally I don't think it is. Somebody doesn't want an honest paper in the city, and whoever it is is going all out to stop me. Here's your chance, Valerie. If you haven't got a mind for schemozzles, step aside before the tractor starts rolling over you — if you have, climb on the merry-go-round, and take your chance of being flung off into a nice cosy coffin.'

'You aren't suggesting . . . ?'

'I am. I think they'll stop at nothing after what happened to Georgia. What say?'

'The merry-go-round's going too fast,' she said.

'You mean you want to duck off?'

'No; I *like* a merry-go-round to go fast,'

she said, looking me full in the eyes.

I slapped her back. 'You're swell. We'll rub along great. And between Jimmy and you and I, we'll rip this whole god-damned island apart!'

We didn't discuss it again after that, and when we were through eating we went along as far as Rollerdrome and got in the jam on the floor.

A 'Gents Only' came round, and Val got off the rink. I stayed on, ready to do my stuff in the whirl.

I noticed the two uglies who were skating along behind me, and suddenly got panicky. Because I recognised them for Leather and his buddy! They didn't seem to have spotted me, however, and it was too late to head off the floor anyway. I had to keep going fast round the rink — I was hemmed in on all sides!

I saw Leather drawing nearer, his pal falling slightly behind. I put on a terrific burst of speed and tried to draw away, but there was a knot ahead of me who weren't moving too fast, and I had to hold back.

Then I got one hell of a shove from the right, staggered for balance, buckled over on my skates, and went down.

I could see guys sweeping all around me, some jumping over me. I saw a pair of iron feet heading right for me as I lay there; and those *didn't* jump!

They battered right into my already-bruised face! Then Leathers' buddy was lying beside me, and through my agony I heard him say: 'Lay off, O'Halloran, or you won't have any pan at all left soon!'

He was gone in the crowd when somebody blew the whistle and they got me off the floor. I didn't start anything; I couldn't spot either Leather or his buddy anywhere. I kept quiet while they bathed my smashed lips and fixed my split cheek. I knew I must look terrible after that last beating, to get injured on top of it again.

Valerie took me home. She came right up to my apartment, came in with me, and made me lie on the settee while she percolated coffee. Then she came back and made me drink some, after which I felt better. She said:

'What rotten luck that was, Larry.'

'Luck, nothing! It was done purposely. I was pushed.'

She looked at me as if she couldn't believe her ears. 'You mean someone did it deliberately?'

'Just that. Whoever this Raven is, he's poison. Any man who has a couple of strong-arm men, like the guys who did this to me, must be dangerous. No, this wasn't any accident. I as good as saw it coming along, but I was too late to get clear. I asked for it. But from here on, I'm walking round armed.'

'Why not tell the police?' she said.

'The cops? You're too innocent to understand, Val. The cops would want concrete proof, and I can't even name the guys. No, I'll bide my time — I've got plenty to bide. I'll be ready for the next move, though. I've taken all I'm going to — next time it'll be *my* turn!'

She looked worriedly down at me, and sighed. 'You will be careful, Larry?'

I grinned at her from behind my fresh selection of bandages. 'You care?'

'You're my meal ticket; why shouldn't I?'

I snorted. I said: 'That's fine! So that's what you think of me.'

She leaned over. She murmured: 'I was only joking. I like you a lot. You will take care?'

'For you, sure. I hope you'll like me a lot more than a lot before we're through.'

'That depends — '

'On what I look like during the infrequent intervals when my pan isn't bruised?'

'No; it depends on you yourself.'

'Don't get it.'

'Don't want you to; you'll see what I mean — or if you don't, you will after a while.'

I relaxed in the chair and she stroked my aching brow with a cool hand.

I must have gone off to sleep right there; when I woke it was ten by the clock on the bedtable. Valerie had gone home, I supposed, and the room was getting chilly. My head and face ached worse than ever, and I was beginning to feel like the ball in a Notre Dame versus Harvard match.

Someone downstairs in the hall buzzed my speaking tube. I reached out and picked it up. I said: 'Yeah?'

'O'Halloran?'

'I guess so. Who is it down there?'

'Dexter — Oswald Dexter. I'd like to see you.'

'Come right on up, and walk in.'

I downed the tube and stared thoughtfully at my fingernails. What in hell could a big bug in the paper world, owner of the *Recorder* and two or three other news-sheets, be doing wanting to see a second-rate reporter like myself? I smelt something that wasn't orchids. I walked into the sitting room and sat.

The door opened and Dexter came in. I don't know if you ever met this mug Dexter, but I can give you a thumbnail sketch right now without disturbing you overmuch.

He is fat; so fat he almost fills the average door. He is big with it, unlike most fat people. By big, I mean tall. But tall!

Lying down in a slope-back chair like I was, I got the notion he was the mountain that didn't come to Mahomet, but was coming to me. He heaved to and cast anchor just above me, and I glanced up and said: 'Take a seat — no charge.'

'Thank you, no. I prefer to stand to say

what I have to say. I prefer it for psychology's sake — it gives me the superiority of the interview.'

'You say so.' I waved. 'But make it brief and brisk. I don't like you and I don't like your face.'

'I can't see your face, but I don't like your manners,' he said in his fruity voice, giving me a glare from pulled-out eyes, and wobbling his three chins dangerously. 'However, I'll overlook them this time. I'm here to ask you to abandon this ridiculous scheme you have for starting your own paper.'

'What inducement?'

'Your own job on the *Recorder* at an increased salary, and a gift of — say — fifty thousand dollars.'

'And you'll print the stuff I bring in? Like, for example, the Ancaster Allan affair?'

'No. I can't agree to that. But if you don't come back for us on my terms, you'll come to grief, O'Halloran — '

I said, briefly and snappily: 'Get out! *Out!*'

6

He didn't get out; he stayed right where he was and fought with his own haughtiness. I could see his face working; I knew he wanted to tell me to get to hell, and beat it, but he didn't.

When he spoke he'd dropped the hard, do-this-or-see-what-you-get tone of voice. His tone was almost wheedling. He said: 'We don't want your competition, O'Halloran, and that's a fact. If you'll let us buy this idea of yours . . . '

'To throw on the scrap heap?' I jeered. 'I get it. You're so scared of a little healthy competition. But you can remedy that by printing public scandals in your own sheet. Why don't you?'

He wasn't anxious to answer that one; he said: 'It's too long a story . . . '

'I got time to spare, O.D.,' I told him. 'I've figured there was something phoney about you for a long time, the way you play down good stories for no reason.

Maybe you'd like to tell me, or take a blasting in the first issue of the *Bombshell*.'

He kneaded dough with his flabby hands, and forgetting all about the psychological advantages of standing, he sat down, his fat rump jamming hard between the arms of one of my chairs. He said:

'I can't tell you anything . . . '

'Nuts. If you *can't*, you needn't *stay*.'

He seemed to make his mind up suddenly. He was afraid of the *Bombshell*, I could see that. Not of its potential sales driving his own sheet to the wall, but of what I might have to say about my own ex-employer and his paper. He said:

'I want you to understand what I'm going to tell you is strictly off the record?'

I nodded; it was either that, or I didn't get to what was back of his actions. I said: 'May I never rate another byline if I use the information.'

He seemed satisfied. I'd worked for him long enough; he knew that when I gave my word, I kept it. He went on:

'You remember the scandal there was

about the four orphan homes outside city limits?'

I thought back, said: 'Let's see. I was a cub then, I guess — five years back, wasn't it? But I seem to recall the more juicy details. What a scoop that was . . . '

'It was. The *Recorder* got it first — but after that first edition every paper in town used the story. They gave, it a two-page spread because of its political significance. The text of it was that the food which was being sold and sent to those out-of-town orphan homes was unfit even for pigs to eat. No wonder half the kids were down ill most of the time. Rotten meat, bad eggs, sides of cattle suffering from foot and mouth, mouldy fruit. Not even the bread they rated was eatable, except by pigs — and perhaps even pigs would have turned their snouts up at some of the stuff those kiddies ate.

'One of our reporters got that scoop; we played it for all we were worth, and the other papers took it up. The authorities were going to content themselves with dismissing the principals, and reprimanding the firm which supplied the goods, the City Caterers & Co., Incorporated. But we kept plugging them for a public enquiry, to see who was *really* getting the graft money.

'That was when we started getting letters; anonymous letters, without addresses, warning us to drop the affair, or something nasty would happen. We laughed at them, myself and the other paper owners; Jake Abard even published his in his paper, the *August*. And you know what happened to Abard . . . '

'He was found shot dead in his home, probably by gangmen.'

'That's right. We didn't connect the warnings with his death right then; we still kept riling the authorities for close investigation — and maybe you can remember what happened next?'

I nodded: 'Every newspaper office in town had a bomb slung at or planted on it!'

'You're darned right it did. The damage done amounted to millions of dollars. And the following day we all received phone calls from this 'Raven', telling us worse would happen if we didn't just hold everything . . . warning us we would go the way Jake Abard went. What could we do? Police? What could *they* do? Uncover the man behind the orphanage scandal? Yes, maybe; but that wouldn't prove *he* was the Raven.

'So we did lay off; it wasn't worth it. We may have been public-spirited, but we weren't public-spirited enough to occupy a nice rosewood casket and rate a two-column obituary in our own paper. We laid off; and once he'd got us, he kept hold — tight. Every now and then a story would break that looked big — and most always we had a call from a gunman, or a letter, or a phone call, telling us to leave the story alone, and to warn our reporters not to touch it.'

'And that's been going on five years? With all of you?'

'Five years. With us all.'

'You mean that out of — lemme see — about five or six big owners right here in Manhattan Island, no one ever had the guts to buck against this guy who entitles himself 'the Raven'?'

'Oh, yes. One man did — over the

Crown-Royal Cinema which collapsed through faulty and cheap materials, and killed thirty kids who were at a matinée. He started to thresh out that story . . . his name was Lester, and he worked on the *Clarion* . . . remember?'

'Yeah. Hit-and-run driver — killed immediately.'

Dexter nodded. And I knew he'd been telling the truth; if you think it's unlikely, even impossible, for six or seven grown men — big noises in the paper world — to be terrorised into the suppression of news, think again. Stranger things have happened; *are* happening, somewhere, right this very minute. But no cheese calling himself anything so melodramatic as 'the Raven' was going to scare me!

Not Lawrence Patrick O'Halloran, they weren't!

'I've told you this,' continued Dexter, rubbing his fat folds of his chin and neck, 'so that you won't go ahead with your hare-brained scheme. So you'll know what's in front of you if you persist. You're the only one besides paper owners who knows the truth about it all. Have

82

some sense before you bark your shins . . . '

'Sorry.' I stood up. 'I'm going on. I'm still going to whale the tar out of your papers and their policies . . . '

'You promised . . . '

'I promised I wouldn't use what you just told me. I won't. But I'll get the information some other way, and use it then. And by the time I'm through, I'll have this Raven in the chair where he belongs by rights. They can't scare me.'

He got up. 'O'Halloran . . . '

'So long, O.D.'

'You're putting your head into a noose . . . '

'I've had it there a long time already, but so far it's not drawn tight enough to choke me off.'

'They've tried?'

'How'd you think I got this pan?'

'Then you know . . . '

'All I know is it's made me more than ever determined to put a stop to the rackets. This Raven must be a big shot . . . '

'He is. I haven't any idea who he is, but

he has a rake-off in most of the crooked things that go on in New York; and I don't mean Manhattan Island alone. I mean the other side of the river, in Brooklyn; and from indications I've seen, he's got a band of stick-at-nothing thugs to back him up.'

'All the more reason why we should stem the rat. Most likely he's a respectable citizen, working alongside us — he could be you, O.D . . . '

Dexter blanched.

'Or even me. He's able to spot everyone's moves in advance, as he can get around openly. But he won't get to know my moves, so that he can't stop them! I'll work blind and alone; I won't even tell my two assistants what my plans are.'

Dexter said: 'You're determined?'

I raised my right hand. 'So help me.'

Dexter dug out his wallet; his chin wobbled. He took out a wad of notes — fifties. About a hundred of them!

'I said I won't be bought off . . . '

'No, no! I admire you for your determination. I'd like you to take these notes to help you . . . there's only one condition: that you don't rap the *Recorder*.'

'You mean . . . '

'Take the starch out of the other sheets all you like; but lay off the *Recorder*. Do that and this wad is for you. And if by any chance, you do get the Raven, there's twice as much in it for you again!'

Maybe, on principle, I should have refused. Maybe — hmmm!

But look at it this way: the main thing was to expose the rottenness in the city; the newspaper angle was a side issue. It wouldn't hurt not to rib the *Recorder*, and the dough would help out with the *Bombshell*. Besides, even after all that had taken place, I still had a soft spot for the old rag. I never did count myself a sentimentalist, but a paper that's employed you for seven years kind of gets its talons in your soft portions. I took O.D.'s filthy lucre and stashed it away in my desk. I said:

'You just bought yourself a whole lot of silence, O.D., as far as the *Recorder* is concerned.'

He didn't say anything else, just nodded, and walked out. I sat back in my chair and reckoned out how much was in hand now. It came out at a little over nine thousand dollars. More than enough to launch the *Manhattan Bombshell*!

★ ★ ★

The first edition hit the boards exactly two weeks after the inception of the idea. And if I say so myself, it was a humdinger! I'd done most of the work myself. The editorial took up the whole of the second page, setting out the future policy of the rag, telling the great American public what suckers they'd been — they love to be told that! — and generally getting down to the rock bottom of what was wrong in this fair city, which was plenty.

The third page of the folder took the form of a résumé of the past cases which had been held out on by the papers. I headed it:

WHY DID THEY HOLD THEIR SILENCE?

and I gave it all I had. I put in as much as I could recall of the cases which had been carefully suppressed, and although it wasn't a whole lot, it sufficed. I couldn't get any further details, for they weren't on file anyplace.

Except maybe police headquarters, and they very often didn't know as much as the reporting boys did.

The back page I gave over to the full details, as I knew them, of the Allan case — not omitting to mention my own beatings-up, and the death of Georgia who'd known too much. I lashed hell out of the police department.

The front page carried banner headlines, reading:

10 Cents
THE MANHATTAN BOMBSHELL
First Burst!

And under that, in type nearly as big:

DO YOU KNOW THIS HANDWRITING?

The handwriting was that on the demand notes addressed to Ancaster Allan. It wasn't any use printing the envelopes, because they were typed out. That made me wonder why the blackmailer hadn't typed the letters too, but I decided it must be personal idiosyncrasy. Anyway, the letters were there, written in a bold, clear hand, but obviously a disguised one. Not that I had much hope of finding out anything from them, but they made sensational reading:

> We are waiting for your further payment of five thousand dollars. We are not prepared to believe that a fine actor like yourself can be short of money. You will kindly follow our directions as usual, and let us have the payment before Wednesday next, or regrettable details of your association with a certain young actress who committed suicide with her unborn child will reach the ears of the general public.
> THE RAVEN!

And embossed on the bottom of the paper was a black Raven!

Glassmer handled his job well; I took a walk round town that same morning to get the lowdown on how the *Bombshell* was selling.

Selling? Hell, I could have charged fifty cents, and it'd still have sold like hot frankfurters on a cold December morning! The first three stalls I tried hadn't a copy left; the next had one or two copies only. The stationers and newsagents were boosting the sales themselves. They'd read the edition and found it good. They recommended it.

Not a copy for sale; but everywhere over town I found guys jaywalking to their offices, reading the *Bombshell* as if their two-cent lives depended on it. The subway trains were full of folks talking their heads off about it all, and the general consensus of opinion was that it was time someone had had the guts to print a paper like it.

There were some who claimed it was just a yellow sheet, got up for sensationalism and big profits; but others said it was worth every cent of the price charged, and that they'd have paid double for it for the privilege of reading the dynamite it held.

When I hit the office again I found I had company in the shape of a large cop. He was sitting twiddling his thumbs in a corner of the outer office, and when I entered, he stood up.

Valerie nodded towards him, said: 'There's a man in uniform to see you over there, Larry.'

'There is?' I said, acting surprised. 'What do you suppose he is? Subway guard?'

'I'm not sure,' she chuckled back, winking. 'At first I thought he might be the iceman, then I decided he looks more like the man who picks up papers in the park.'

I turned round to the red-faced cop who was shuffling his dogs. He growled: 'You can cut out your funny act; and you too, sister. The D.A. wants to see you, O'Halloran.'

'Swell. Swell. I want to see the D.A.'

'You will, don't worry. There's a patrol car outside.'

'So we do it in style, do we? But — hold it, one second.'

He held it. I picked the phone up. I

dialled the D.A.'s office. 'That Coleman? Leslie Coleman, the District Attorney?'

'Talking.'

'O'Halloran this end. Did you send a beefy cop over here for me? Looks like he was wearing last year's model in uniforms?'

'Sure, that's my man. I sent him for you. I'm itching to have a word or two with you, O'Halloran. And bring over those demand notes you claim were sent to Ancaster Allan. I want them.'

'Okay. Be right along.'

I slammed the receiver down on its rest, turned to the cop.

'Let's go, Cuthbert.'

He was peeved. Said: 'Can't you take a man's word?'

'Sure, a *man's* I can. Not a cop's. I have to be careful. I've just touched off a keg of dynamite and I happen to be sitting right on top of it. I have to be ready to jump off in case it explodes.'

'What's that to do with me taking you to the D.A.?'

'How do I know *you* aren't a crook in disguise?'

91

'Can't you tell the difference between a crook and a cop?' he howled, cut up.

'Nope. There isn't any. Let's go. I wouldn't want to keep the D.A. waiting, not for anything.' I turned to Valerie and smiled.

'Trouble's a-brewing, sugar. But keep your fingers crossed. If I don't get back by tonight, phone the cops, and tell them the D.A.'s holding me for nothing. So long.'

She grinned at me, then we went out . . .

7

Coleman, the D.A., was waiting for me in his office at headquarters. He greeted me easily enough, and invited me to take a seat.

'Brought the letters?'

I handed them over to him and waited until he'd studied them. He read them first of all; then he looked at them up and down, sidewise, back to front, and held to the light. He said:

'They look genuine. *Are* they?'

'Mr. Coleman,' I said, shocked. 'You don't think I'd *manufacture* evidence, surely?'

'Don't I? Hmm. Garry — test those for prints. Take O'Halloran's along with you — they're bound to be on.'

A plainclothes fingerprint man took my prints, then left. The D.A. said: 'How'd you get these letters?'

'I found them,' I told him. I knew I was stepping for trouble if I said I'd burgled them out of Georgia Dean's apartment. He said:

'Found them where?'

'In my mailbox — someone must have posted them to me.'

'Any idea who'd want to do that?'

'Not the faintest.'

'Did you get these before or *after* Allan's death?'

'After . . . two weeks ago to be exact.'

'Why didn't you turn them in?'

'You might not have permitted me to use them in my first issue.'

He dropped the subject just like that; that was his way. I knew him, Coleman. Knew his methods. I knew he might shoot back to it at any minute, hoping to catch me out in the confusion. He said:

'What made you think Georgia Dean was shot down because she knew too much?'

'She did know too much. She intended to tell it to me; she'd already given me one signed statement about Allan.'

'I read about that in your paper. Someone took it from you when you got beaten up, didn't they?'

'Exactly. Two mugs, one nicknamed Leather, by way of being an expert on knocking a guy's front teeth to the back of his throat with a short leather strop or thong.'

'They warned you to lay off?'

'They did. Very energetically. Then grabbed the statement.'

'Why hadn't you brought the statement to us in the first place?'

'I got it as a signed article for my paper, the *Recorder*.'

'And why didn't *they* use it?'

'You can ask Oswald Dexter that one. He should know; he banned anything on the Allan case.'

'So you threw your job in, did you? Why didn't you bring us the statement when your sheet turned it down?'

'I meant to at first; then I decided I'd try to get Georgia to spill more of what she knew.'

'You thought she did know more?'

'Sure. I went to see her at the theatre.'

'So we found out from the doorman. Then you left with her.'

'Exactly.'

'Where were you when she was gunned?'

'Right beside her on the floor, hugging the sidewalk.'

'They tried for you too?'

I nodded. He whipped out: 'I suggest that you took her out in that alley specially so's someone you knew could gun her!'

'You're talking through the hole in your neck your collar stud must have made,' I told him. 'Don't try and get me rattled, it won't work. I didn't know a thing about it. I'm on the other side.'

He smiled and tapped his desk. He said: 'You gave us a bit of a rough passage in your article, didn't you? Did a lot of polite sneering at us?'

'Which you deserved.'

'You think so? You may want us to do you a favour one of these days. So far we've made it easy for you to publish your corny paper, but there're licences, permits — we could make it very awkward. You'll admit that?'

I stood up. I said: 'This is a free country. The press is free. If that isn't so, then what am I paying my taxes for?

Okay! So long as you guys are my servants, I feel entitled to take a poke at you now and then. I said you didn't look farther than the ends of your noses, and you don't. If a thing looks like it's a simple case of this, that or the other, you let it go, right or wrong.'

'Why should we go getting involved in complications which would most likely prove to be wrong? If a man kills himself, and it's an obvious suicide, why try to make it murder?'

'You don't have to try that — but why not try to find out *why* he killed himself?'

He smiled lazily. He said: 'We leave that to snoopy reporters!'

I sat down again. The fingerprint man brought a folder in and laid it on the desk before him. He looked it over.

He said: 'That's funny.'

'What is?' I snorted.

He looked me right in the eyes. He murmured: 'There are, on this letter purporting to come from the Raven, two sets of prints. One set belongs to you — and the other . . . to Georgia Dean!'

I shuffled uncomfortably. He said: 'You

told us these were sent to you, didn't you?'

'Did I?' I said blandly. 'Then they must have been.'

'If they were sent, why? Why couldn't this Georgia Dean have handed them over to you, long as she knew you?'

'How should I know that?'

'Hmm. Besides your own prints and the Dean girl's, which are fainter, this report states there is another set, too faint to to be traceable even if we had the duplicates to them. Whose do you suppose those could be?'

'Ancaster Allan's, I expect. I daresay Georgia got the letters from him before she sent them on to me.'

'You think he gave them to her?'

'Maybe.'

The D.A. looked sceptical. I lit a cigarette. He rapped: 'I'm investigating murder. Put out that smoke and pay attention or you'll find yourself inside.'

'On what charge?' I grunted.

'Suppression of material evidence'll do until I get something better.'

I put out the smoke. He was feeling tough; he wasn't to be argued with right now. I'd done all the ribbing he was going to stand for. He leaned forward and fixed his eyes on my face.

'Come clean, O'Halloran! You know more than this?'

'Not a thing, Mr. Coleman, so help me.'

He stood up; said: 'Do we have to grill you?'

'You can if you feel you'd ease yourself any by it. But you couldn't learn anything more than I've told you. I don't know any more than that.'

'What's your racket in starting this paper?'

'To crush this guy who calls himself the Raven. It beats me why the public haven't heard of him before. He seems to be mixed up in a whole lot of things in Manhattan.'

'We've heard of him,' ventured Coleman. 'And what's more, he's a very tough merchant. We don't know who he is — nor do most of his boys. I expect he conveys instructions to them through an intermediary. We've caught a few of them, extorting money from shopkeepers. The old protection racket. But they never talk. They choose to go in and do their spell.'

'I see; I didn't know you'd been working on the case. Sorry I slated you. I'll lay off your department in future, Mr. Coleman.'

'You'd better O'Halloran. Better lay off all the city departments, for that matter. We might get tougher than this. I'm not sure that I shouldn't hold you now.'

'What good would that do you? I'm best left alone. Best left to run my rag — sooner or later this Raven'll try to get me, and then you'll have your chance!'

He pursed his lips. He said: 'That's so. There's one thing — you'll agree to keep us informed of anything . . . unusual?'

'I agree to that. If there is anything I think you should know, I'll see you hear from me.'

'Not anything *you think* we should know — just anything we *should* know. You can go, O'Halloran. I'm keeping these notes — and I want you to send me the envelopes you received them in.'

'I can't. They came together. I burnt the envelope.'

'Conveniently, eh?'

'I'll compromise. I'll send you the

envelopes they were sent to Ancaster Allan in. Okay?'

'I suppose so.'

I walked out of the office grinning. Coleman was one of the toughest bozos to crack in the whole of the Department of Justice. The fact that he'd taken it so easy with me told me one thing. He thought someone would try to get me; thought I'd find out something else on the case; thought I'd held out on him. He would have me followed, I knew that. He'd set his shadows on my trail, and keep tabs on my every movement.

How right I was! I knew long before I'd covered half the distance to my own office. Accordingly, I walked calmly in the portals of a super hotel.

I waited patiently until I saw the two red-faced, somewhat stout, myrmidons of the force come in after me, trying to look inconspicuous and defeating their purpose by their obvious efforts. I went across the hall fast, past the desk clerk, and they hurried after me. I slid in a lift just as the doors began to close, saw them stop dead and stare.

Then they sprinted for the stairs!

They didn't dare to take another lift; I might have stepped off at any floor, and they wouldn't have known. They had to sprint from floor to floor, checking whether or not I'd got off.

I went right up to the sixtieth, got off, and lounged coolly against the head of the staircase, waiting and smoking. Eventually they came into view, puffing and perspiring, their bowler hats pushed loosely to the back of their square heads. They spotted me, leaning nonchalantly there, paused, grunted; then, affecting to ignore me, walked past and along the passage. Here they pretended to be looking for a room number.

I walked across to them. I said cheerfully: 'Can I help you gentlemen?'

'Uh — er — yup — well, we were trying to find the suite numbered eighty — er — three.'

'You were? Then I *can* help you. It's on the next floor up.'

'The — er — next floor?' said the first one.

'That's it.'

'Hem — up?' questioned the second.

'Precisely.'

'Then we must have been mistaken,' said the first, smitten with a sudden brainwave. 'This is the floor we want I know. We must have the wrong number. We'll wait here — for a friend of ours. I expect he'll be coming home shortly, and he's bound to pass along here.'

'If you're certain.'

'Oh, sure. We are.'

'Very well. Only *I* could have shown you said eighty-three. I'm on my way up myself. Goodbye, gentlemen.'

I started up the stairs leaving them gawking stupidly after me. I hit the next floor and peered back. Two furtive hats were edging cautiously round the corner of the stairs. I grinned and drew back. They came up. I stepped towards them.

'It was this floor after all, eh?' I said.

'Yes, yes. This — er — floor. Hmm.'

'Eighty-three?'

'Yes.'

'There it is, then. Hadn't you better try it?'

They looked helplessly at each other,

then at my questioning stare. The first said: 'I — er — don't think so.'

'But you wanted it? Really, what are you two up to? This is beginning to look extremely suspicious to me.'

They shrugged helplessly and walked towards eighty-three. The D.A. must have enforced it on them that they had not to let me know they were following me. I grinned. They were too thick to see I was pulling their plain-clothed legs for all I was worth. They were going to try and bluff it out, even to knocking at a stranger's door.

They knocked. I said: 'Try the buzzer — maybe they can't hear you. You didn't rap very loud.'

They grunted and thumbed the buzzer. The door opened and a young golden-haired girl in a negligée stared out.

She snapped: 'Yes?'

'We — er — that is . . . '

'That is what?' she said sharply. 'What's the idea?'

I slid along to a service phone at the end of the passage.

I got on to the desk clerk, said: 'There's

a pair of mashers trying to molest the young lady in eighty-three. Send the house dick along at once.'

Meanwhile, the argument at eighty-three was developing. The girl wasn't giving them any chance to get a word in edgeways.

'I know your game,' she snorted. 'Prowlers! Peeping Toms! There's a law about your sort. How dare you ring people's buzzers for no reason at all?'

'We must have been mis — '

'Mistaken, nothing! This is the only suite at this end of the floor. You came here deliberately. I've heard of men like you two who sneak up on innocent girls living alone and trying to like it! Wolves! Sugar daddies! Mashers! I want to know . . . '

The elevator jarred to a halt and a squat, stubbly man got out. He breezed rapidly along past me to the door of eighty-three, thumbs hitched in vest armholes. He eyed the two detectives with suspicion. He said: 'What's the game? You guys don't live here. I've half a mind to run you in. What you want?'

'We'll explain . . . later . . . '

'Later, nothing. Explain now and make it good.'

'Here, take a look at this,' muttered one, with a furtive stare in my direction. He held out his police card in the palm of his hand. The house dick stared, then yelped: 'Why didn't you say you was — '

'*Shhh!*' hissed the detectives, glaring at him; I grinned and started to skip rapidly down the stairs. I was fresh and energetic; I covered the stairs at a great rate. In ten minutes I was down in the hall, waiting for the 'tecs. I was sitting on a settee, my face hidden behind a newspaper, when they came panting down. I poked a hole with my smoke, peered through. They were hot and unhappy, sweating at every pore, and probably hating the life they led. They walked over and plumped into the seats next to me, thinking I must have ducked out. I heard one say: 'Hell! The D.A.'ll blow us up for this. The rat skipped out on us!'

'Yeah. After all the trouble we took, too. D'you suppose he had an idea we were following him?'

'Naw! Couldn't have. We played it

along, didn't we? How could he have guessed? We don't look like detectives, do we? No, he didn't know it was him we we tailing about.'

'But he ducked us like he did.'

'Sure, coincidence. That's all. Where do we look for him now?'

I folded the paper and put it away; I leaned over and said, very confidentially: 'Are you saps — sorry, boys — looking for Larry O'Halloran of the *Bombshell*?'

'Why, sure, that's it — we — *hey! You're O'Halloran!*'

'I hope so.' I grinned at them. 'I'm hopping in a taxicab now, fellers; if you need me, I'm heading right for the *Bombshell* offices — I guess you know the address. And next time you see the D.A., tell him I'm highly honoured to have a personal bodyguard all to myself; especially such an intelligent bodyguard!'

I got up and left them staring after me; they seemed fed up to the back teeth, but they had their jobs to do. By the time I'd reached my office they were after me again, this time throwing caution to the wind!

8

'Hello,' greeted Valerie, looking up as I entered. 'Wish you'd been her today — we've been worn to a frazzle with phone calls from people who've read your stuff in the *Bombshell*.'

'People?'

'Mmm. Ever since you left with that policeman they've been 'phoning in — some wanting to buy advert space . . . plenty of those. What do I tell them?'

It was a sore temptation; sell space and make a fortune. Make the *Bombshell* eight or twelve times the size it was — no! Then it would become just another daily. I said: 'Tell them we don't print anything but big news. Sorry.'

'Then there've been lots of people wanting to congratulate you on your first issue — including a man called Dexter . . . '

'Oswald Dexter?' I asked, interested.

'That was the name.'

'My, my, we are becoming famous. Anything else?'

'Oh, yes. Quite a few nasty calls, from people who think you ought to be hanged or shot or possibly drawn and quartered.'

I nodded. 'I expected a certain amount of that; some guys just don't like having their equanimity disturbed. They think New York is God's own city, and themselves God's chosen people, and the mere suggestion that there might be something rotten in this place gets them all steamed up. Forget about calls like those, and if you think any call you take is heading that way just hang up. Anything more?'

She pondered; said: 'There was a person — a man, who was very insistent on talking to you. I told him to call back.'

'Okay. Where's Jimmy?'

'Out covering a local killing again.'

I went through into the inner office, sat down at the typewriter, and started dribbling a little tentative stuff out. I had only done a page or so when the phone rang. I picked it up.

'Hello?'

'Mr. O'Halloran?'

'The great man himself.'

'Excellent. 'Once upon a midnight dreary, while I pondered, weak and weary . . . ' — does that tell you who's speaking at this end, Mr. O'Halloran?'

' 'Take thy beak from out my heart, and take thy form from off my door!'' I quoted back. 'Poe's 'The Raven'. What d'you want, Raven?'

'Another little warning, Mr. O' Halloran. But this time it's final. Your very last. Take one more step towards poking your nose into my business, and *bang* goes the *Bombshell*!'

'You must be worried, Raven. I'd like to see you and talk it over some.'

He chuckled; deep tones. Said: 'So would a lot of people like to see me, Mr. O'Halloran. But they'll all be disappointed, I think. You take notice of my warning, and you'll come to no harm . . . '

'Nuts. I go on . . . and if I don't manage to get rid of you, you melodramatic louse, I'll . . . '

He cut in: 'Remember the end of the poem 'The Raven'?'

110

I did. I started to speak. He said: "'And the Raven, never flitting, still is sitting / On the pallid bust of Pallas just above my chamber door; / And his eyes have all the seeming of a demon's that is dreaming / And the lamp-light o'er him streaming throws his shadow on the floor; / And my soul from out that shadow that lies floating on the floor / Shall be lifted — nevermore!'"

'You're nuts!' I said briefly, and hung up on him. But I was very thoughtful. I didn't try to trace the call, because he was smart enough to take care I couldn't. But the call had worried me, and then some. I had thought he used the alias of the Raven because it was as good as any name, and implied a bird of ill omen, which he undoubtedly was. But — and the *but* was a big one! — I knew an educated man with a fancy for Poe's Raven, who styled himself after the bird in that piece of gloomy, macabre writing, would be a dangerous enemy.

Crooks are just crooks; but when they go round acting like the guy on the phone had just acted, they are also a little wacky.

And being a little wacky in that way makes them far worse enemies than the ordinary small-time, uneducated thug. He was fond of melodrama, and he had imagination; that made him, in my eyes, perilous.

Dangerous or not, though, I wasn't backing out now. No sir, I was in for better or for worse, and if I didn't fleece the feathers of that Raven before I was much older, I'd throw the paper game over altogether.

I found some reassurance in the fact that I could, looking from the window, see the stout figures of my shadows perambulating up and down the sidewalk. I decided that they might be useful sooner or later. But not for my next move. Somehow I had to get rid of them. I didn't want the D.A. to know what line I was following; he might blunder round himself and frighten my bird of prey off!

I went into the outer office. I said to Valerie: 'How good can you get excited?'

'In what way?' she smiled.

'Would it worry you much if you found me throttled in the office?'

She paled: 'Are you expecting me to?'

'I wouldn't be surprised. Would it worry you?'

She lay a hand on mine, said: 'I think I'd go mad. You know I'd go mad!'

'That's swell. You do think a small portion of me then?'

She chuckled. She said: 'You're still my bread and butter!'

'Okay, I asked for it. But could you put on a convincing act for two gentlemen from the Department of Justice?'

She nodded: 'What do you want me to do?'

'Dash out into the street, down below. Rush over to the two fat ginks who are hanging round out there, tell them you've just found Mr. O'Halloran's corpse in the inner office. Say he was strangled. Can you do that convincingly?'

'I'll try. What then?'

'Bring them up here in the elevator. Not by the stairs, because I'll be going down by the stairs, and I'm very anxious to lose them!'

She smiled: 'And what do I tell them when they find out there isn't a body?'

'Just say: 'Well, whaddaya know! One of them vanishing corpses! Sorry you've been troubled, boys.''

'Won't they be mad?' she asked, dubiously.

'As hell. But you needn't let that worry you. They'll tumble it was a gag, but they can't touch you. And if they ask, you've no idea where I could be. Okay?'

She held thumb and forefinger up, pressed together in an okay sign. I chucked her under the chin, kissed her gently on the cheek, and said: 'Make with the hysterics, baby!'

I watched her from the window, and it was sure a sight for sore eyes. She came running out, gazed helplessly around as if looking for a policeman, then dashed over to the two dicks. I saw her gesturing frantically towards the office windows, talking rapidly and disjointedly. The two dicks jumped, then followed her, starting at a trot across the road and then disappearing into the doorway.

I got my dogs galloping and slid out of the office. Just to make things harder for them, I locked the door so's they'd have trouble getting in. I hit the stairs and travelled down them fast. I could hear the elevator going up, and I grinned to myself. Those two cops were going to be extremely disappointed when they didn't find any corpse up there — but what the hell? That's a thing cops have to get used to, according to the movies. Murdered men nearly always vanish!

I was vanishing, anyway. Fast. I did the forty floors down in record time, and if there'd been a record for sprinting up and down a forty story building I reckon I'd have broken it.

I gained the street and flagged a crawling cab; as I was getting in I spotted two red and wrathful faces gawking out of the office windows far above. I waved cheerfully to them, gave the cabby the address, and piled in.

We shot out into Midtown Manhattan, through the teeming traffic; my destination was the offices of the *Recorder*. I didn't work for the paper anymore but I meant to make it work for me. I got off outside and walked right in, nodding to the commissionaire. He didn't attempt to stop me, he knew me too well.

I didn't go near the editorial department, or the newsroom. The boys would be in there getting copy out, and I didn't want anyone to know I was in the building — not anyone who might have told the chief. I made right for the filing room, and found it empty except for Old Alec, who keeps the files.

'Howdy, Alec,' I told him, taking a seat. 'How's the rheumatism treating you there days?'

'Something awful, Mr. O'H.,' he grumbled. 'But what are you doing here? You don't work here anymore?'

'Not any more, Alec. But I fancied you might care to earn five bucks?'

'I expect I might.'

'I'm anxious to look through the records of the *Recorder* for five years back. Can do?'

'I think so — yes. You know where to find them. Help yourself.'

I filched the books out and started running through the news sections. I found what I wanted on page one of the edition for May the first. I read it quickly and jotted down notes in my book. Two addresses, with names. One was Miss N.M.L. Lang, matron, Oakdene Orphan Home; and the other Miss Gayna Beesly, Elmview ditto. There were six homes involved in the orphan scandal, but the article only gave the names of those two of the dismissed principals. Those would do to start with. I slid my book away. I stood up. I gave Old Alec five bucks and added another five on top. I said: 'That's so's you'll forget I was even here today, let alone what I looked at. I'm mighty eager to keep my actions dark from a certain bird of ill omen!'

He looked puzzled but said nothing. I knew he wouldn't give me away at that.

I took another cab outside; if those two flatties were still on the trail, I wasn't giving them any rest. I got out at Grand Central and went into a public payphone. I looked through the directory for the Ls. I found Lang. There were plenty of Langs — hundreds of them all over town. No easy job to find the one I wanted. Besides, in five years there might have been any amount of things happening. She might now be a Mrs. Something without a private phone number, she might have left New York after that orphan home scandal, or she just might not have a phone at all. But I had to try.

And at last I found it — N.M.L. Lang (Miss), and an address in the Bronx of all places. The frail must have gone from bad to worse!

I tried for Gayna Beesly, also; might as well have a second line to fall back on in case the first proved hopeless. But there wasn't a solitary Gayna Beesly in the book. I decided she must have left the town or gotten herself married off to someone without any sense. I say without any sense, because anyone who helps graft money by giving poor little kids rotten food is no fit wife for any decent citizen.

I skipped out of the booth, piled aboard my taxi again, gave him the address of this N.M.L. Lang.

It wasn't as bad a neighbourhood as I'd thought when I'd read her Bronx address. It was old-type: iron lacework balconies, on houses which had been converted into apartment blocks. It was, anyway, free of the hordes of yelling kids which usually infest the joint. I found her door along one of the balconies, knocked. It opened at once and a feller looked out at me.

He wouldn't have been crowned Mr. America at any competition. He had a large flat pan, with stalky eyes and a bulbous snout. His chin as like a scrap of coarse sandpaper, and I could picture him trimming his nails up on his sideboards. His teeth were the kind that look better when the lips are closed over them, and his hair was a thing of the past. The top of his bald dome was yellow.

I looked at him; he looked at me.

And right away something seemed to say to me: *Larry, boy, here's where you get your ears knocked back if you aren't careful with the pretty gentleman.*

He grunted: 'What you want, mister?'

I put on a winning smile. I said: 'I'm looking for a Miss N.M.L. Lang. Could you help me?'

'Help you? Just tell me what you want with Nora, an' then I'll tell you whether I could help you or not.'

'Well, I'd like to interview her — for

— for my paper the *Bombshell*.'

He stared hard at me. He said: 'Is there any money in it?'

'Ten dollars for the interview,' I hazarded.

He opened the door and said: 'Come in, mister. Nora went out, but she'll back be shortly.'

I went in, and he nodded me over towards a derelict chair.

He said: 'Nora is out right now. Maybe I could tell you something?'

'I think not. It's something that happened in the past. Thanks just the same.'

He was in a conversational mood. He went on: 'She's a good girl, is Nora. Known her four years now — she looks after me. I can't get to do no work, I can't. I ain't so strong like I used to be. Nora works for us both.'

'She's your wife?'

'No. I don't believe in marriage. Neither does Nora. What were you wanting to see her about?'

'It's maybe something you don't know about.' I told him. 'When she was matron or superintendent, or what have you, at

120

the Oakdene Orphan Asylum.'

He had stiffened in his chair. He said: 'What do you mean? Are you going to rake up all that stuff again?'

'No, no,' I said hastily. 'It — er — it's just routine work, not for use in the paper.'

'You just said it was for use in your paper?'

'I — I wasn't thinking.'

He got up; he said: 'Maybe you better go, mister. Nora's got no use for hearing about all that old stuff what happened years ago. She'll be proper real mad if she you catches here. You better go.'

He was walking slowly towards me; I got up keeping my eye on his ham-like hands. I knew what touchy cusses guys like him could be. I said: 'I've got to have this information . . . '

'You don't have to get anything from Nora. An' you don't have to forger the ten dollars you promised me . . . '

I started to get mad, and though I tried to control myself I couldn't. I cursed the hot-headed streak in me; if I started anything with this rough, it was a cert he'd be the one to finish it. But the idea of him trying to prise me loose of ten bucks for an interview I hadn't even had, riled me good and plenty.

I snapped: 'Ten bucks your Aunt Fanny. I'm giving no ten bucks away for nothing, pal, so get wise.'

'You get wise,' he growled. 'And hand over that ten bucks, or else, maybe, I get tough!'

'Not with me, brother,' I said, and simultaneously made a jump for the door — to find he'd locked it after me!

He came over and got a hand round my throat; he shook me 'til my teeth rattled. He growled: 'You owe me ten bucks!'

'Leggo, you swine, I'll . . . let . . . you have it!'

I drove my knee into his groin; pain flared in his eyes; his hand began to tighten, strangling me, while I struggled helplessly against him. I kicked out again, rabbit-punched the base of his skull. He roared, landed a fist like rock on my ear, hurling me aside. Then he came for me, flicking open a pocket knife . . .

9

He'd lost all control of himself; he meant business with that knife, and he wasn't going to bother thinking about any consequences, either. It would have been just too bad for your favourite reporter if the door hadn't flown open, unlocked from outside, at that very minute; and a girl — or maybe I should say woman — stepped in.

Her eyes took in the scene at a glance; she seemed to react without showing panic. I got the idea maybe she'd had trouble with this lug she lived with before.

She snapped: 'Gustav! Don't do that — keep your temper!'

He slobbered through his thick lips and glared at her too; she said: 'Gustav — the police will electrocute you!'

That shook him; the glare faded out of his peepers, the knife dropped to his side, and he slunk over to his chair and sat down. She walked forward, and I muttered:

'Thanks, sister. Though why you want a crazy guy like him round anyway beats me.'

He must have heard my crack, and I wished I hadn't let it slip when he rumbled in his throat and started to get up.

The woman looked at him, said: 'Go into the other room, Gustav. At once!'

He hesitated; then, like a naughty dog with its tail between its legs, he beat it, giving me a sullen glare as he went. The woman sighed wearily and laid down a shopping bag. She said: 'You shouldn't have irritated him — he has a foul temper when he's roused.'

'You're telling me,' I grunted, feeling the bruises round my neck. 'The mutt wants putting away someplace. I shouldn't think even you are safe in the house alone with him.'

'I'm not — but — ' She paused. Then said: 'It's glandular trouble. It only came on him these last three years. Before that, he was different altogether. I loved him — I don't want to see him go into an asylum. Not yet.'

I gazed at her with a new respect.

Whatever else she might be, she was certainly loyal to stick that guy and his moods. And to work for him. A dame like that couldn't be all bad, even if she had had a hand in feeding kiddies under her control lousy grub. She said:

'Who are you, anyway?'

'The name's O'Halloran. If you're Nora Lang, I'm looking for you.'

'I'm Nora Lang all right. What was it you wanted?'

I paused. I didn't know how she was going to react to my question. I decided to start easy; I said: 'I'm looking into a company called the City Caterers A.I. Co., Inc.'

'Are you?'

That didn't sound promising, but I persevered: 'That's right. Now, I understand you had some dealings with them when you were matron of Oakdene Orphan Home?'

She was a hard-featured dame, and her make-up hadn't done a thing to soften her looks. Her figure was hard and angular, and if she was a woman who had to have a man, I could understand her sticking to Gussy, even if he was half-touched. If she'd lost him, she'd have had ahard job to find another guy. Her face had gone even harder at my words, and she said: 'I've heard enough about what I did at Oakdene. It's brought me to this.'

'You'd like to earn a few bucks, though?'

She hesitated. She said: 'How many?'

'I'll make it twenty if you can tell me anything that counts.'

'What did you want to know?'

I leaned back; she was seemingly willing to steel herself to having a little chat about Oakdene, even if it did hurt her to hear it talked about.

'How come you and those other five superintendents came to give the kids bum food?'

'It was suggested to us, I believe. Gayna Beesly, who ran the Elmview Home, arranged it all through a man she was friendly with. His name was Barney — I didn't know his other.'

'So you just took the bad grub and got a rake-off?'

'That's so.'

'This Barney — what was he like?'

'A typical gangster — rough-looking. He always went about with a friend called Leather.'

I sat up; things were beginning to break. I said: 'This guy Leather — did you ever see him toting a leather thong round with him?'

'Yes; often, when they came with the vans of food.'

'There was someone else behind them, wasn't there?'

'Someone called the Raven — only Barney knew just who he was. He never spoke of him to anyone.'

'Was he anything to do with the City Caterers A.I. Co.?'

'I think so. When the game was exposed by a reporter from the *Recorder*, the City Caterers closed up soon after. They got away with a reprimand, but the top man was never revealed.'

'Then they just vanished, huh?' She nodded. I said: 'I guess that was because whoever was top man was afraid of there being an investigation.'

'I expect so. I was fired. And that's about all I can tell you. Is it worth the twenty?'

I peeled twenty off my roll. I added ten. I said: 'Ten more if you can say where I might contact this Gayna Beesly who ran the Elmview Home?'

She looked thoughtful. Said: 'I haven't seen Gayna for years. But she used to go quite a lot to the Casino Club in Harlem. She was fond of that place, and Barney used to hang out there too. Maybe, if she's still in Manhattan, she still does go.'

I flipped her the thirty bucks. I said: 'Thanks, Nora. Don't say I've been here to anyone, or your life isn't worth a bent cent. And here's a buck extra — buy a collar and chain for your watchdog!'

★ ★ ★

I didn't get along to the Casino Club until two days later. There was a lot of work to do for the next edition, and Jimmy Edwards wasn't able to handle it all. And everywhere that Larry went, those two fat clunks from Divisional

Headquarters were sure to go as well!

I got used to them following me around, and wondered when they'd be recalled. They weren't recalled. Obviously the D.A. was staking a lot on me providing some kind of lead for him.

They were outside the Casino Club when I went in and lost myself in the whirling crowd on the stamp-size dance floor. I found me a table in an obscure position, and gained the attention of a waitress by the simple expedient of slapping her hard on the part which is last to go through a door.

She flashed a row of white teeth, wiped off the table on to my lap, and said: 'What can I get for you?'

I showed her the colour of a buck, and said: 'I'm wanting to know if a dame called Gayna Beesly comes here still?'

'Miss Beesly?' she said, looking surprised. 'Why, sure. But you don't want no truck with that one. Mr. Barney'd kill any man who tried to steal Miss Gayna off him.'

'Let me be the judge of that,' I said, handing the buck to her and watching her tuck it away. 'There any chances of Miss Beesly being here tonight, maybe?'

She nodded. 'Reckon she'll be around later on,' she told me. 'Tall lady with red hair, an' generally wears a green dress. I'll point her out to you, sir, if you wish.'

'Do,' I said. 'And to be going along with, what you got to drink?'

'Make you a Casino special?' she asked.

'That poison?'

'Sure is.'

'Then it'll do.' I watched her carve a way through the tables towards the bar, and glanced idly round until she'd returned with the drink. It was green, and thick, and I wondered what in hell it was composed of. I could smell peppermint, and that was harmless enough; but it wasn't all peppermint by a long way. There was a richer, smoother smell to it. I shut my eyes, held my snoot, and tipped it down.

Right away I heard a brass band begin to play, a shaft of pure sunlight blazed through the roof, and I had to hold my head with my hands to make sure it didn't float right away. I wiped away an involuntary tear from my eye, and drained the rest.

I began to get a good idea of what the 'Frisco earthquake must have felt like to anyone in it. The room began to spin and spin, and I felt like I was spinning with it, and the band blared out into my ears so that I jammed my hands over them and tried to shut out the sounds; and then I started feeling sick, and got to my feet and lurched towards the door at a stumbling run. I didn't make it.

Halfway there I lost my guts!

I retched like hell, not caring much what folk thought about it all. I wished to tarnation I was good and dead, and not able to feel like I felt, as if there was a large electric fan whirling round in my insides. And then my head went, too, and I started canting over towards the floor, towards the small circle the dancers had left for me. It seemed a long long time coming up to me, that floor. Nobody moved or yelled, so I guess it couldn't have been that long, but it seemed it to me.

I saw the boards sloping obliquely

towards me, heard myself say: 'Hellfire!' and saw a gaping circle of faces round me. Then I hit and lay still, trying to keep my guts where they ought to keep.

Two guys walked over; one said: 'Move aside, folks. The guy passed out. We'll take him in back and revive him some.'

I didn't realise until then that they'd slipped me a concentrated Mickey! Boy, what a dope I was! Here I'd walked in and told the waitress who I was looking for, and she'd likely told someone else, and some sonofabitch had arranged to have me neatly taken care of like this! What a dope I was!

I felt myself being lifted, and my skull was getting ready to burst in two separate halves at any minute — whether it did or not I don't know, because right at that point I passed out with only a twittering of birds in my ears, and a couple of hydraulic drills at work in my head!

I might act smart, but at heart I was just another sucker!

★ ★ ★

I don't know how long I was out, but it was some time, I guess. I dreamed some pretty rotten dreams, too; I was in a jungle someplace, and a hot sun was beating down on me so that I had to shut my glims tight against the fierce heat of it. From a tree over my head a monkey was swinging; and when I got a load of his pan, it bore a strong resemblance to Nora Lang's man Gustav. I ducked out from under as it made a swipe at me, but found I could only duck so far — I stuck there, somehow, while the monkey gibbered and shrieked and yelled at me, and kept sending stinging slaps across my face. The sun beat down and down and nearly drove me mad, and I squirmed and groaned to get away from under it.

I came round.

Some cuss was slapping the hell out of my face; above my head was a strong light, beating right down into my eyes. I was tied in a chair, tied with my wrists behind the back of it. It was a straight-backed dining-room chair, and it was shoved near to a table, with the strong lamp shining towards me, and leaving the other side of the table in darkness and shadows.

I blinked my peepers open, kept them open this time, screwing them up against the glare of the lamp. There was a guy stood on either side of me: one was Barney, the other Leather. Leather had his thong in his hands! There was a dame seated off to one side manicuring her nails, carefully. She had red hair and a tall, slim body, and she wore a green dress. She might have been anywhere between twenty-eight and thirty-eight. You couldn't tell.

I guessed that was Barney's dame, Gayna.

I said: 'Hiya, fellers.'

Barney grunted: 'So you came around, huh? I been slapping your pan for the last ten minutes.'

'It *feels* like you have,' I agreed. 'Did you have to be so tough about it?'

'It ain't anything to what you're going to get when we've had our orders,' croaked Leather. 'The Raven's coming.'

I glanced at Barney. Barney said: 'That's right. I sent for him when you walked into the place. What a sap you are, putting yourself right into our hands, O'Halloran. You saved us plenty of trouble going after you.'

I said: 'How long'll he be?'

'About five foot eleven,' grinned the dame, speaking for the first time, and trying to be funny.

I cracked back: 'When'd they mislay you from the Bob Hope programme, sister?'

She got up and came over; she slapped my face so it hurt. She said: 'Don't be smart, mister. You aren't in the position.'

Barney said: 'Let the guy alone. He's got plenty to come.'

'Shut up, Barney,' she snapped. 'I'm not letting any sap make fun of my jokes.'

'It was a bit corny,' said Barney, reasonably. 'I heard Cantor use it years ago. You're too fond of trying to be funny.'

'Why, you . . . ' she began, then caught his eye and stopped.

He said: 'Sit down, Gayna . . . Sid-down!'

She sat down, quick. There was a mean look in Barney's eye, the same look he'd worn when he'd crashed his skates into my face at the rink that night. Gayna seemed to know it well, and shied away from it. I made conversation to while time away. I said:

'How many rackets are you guys tangled in?'

Leather said: 'Most all of them, sucker. The Raven's a clever feller. You should've kept your nose clean.'

'You were running the City Caterers A.I. Co., when the orphan scandal blew up?' I went on, inquisitively.

'That's right,' Barney said.

'How about the cinema that collapsed on the kids at a matinée performance? Was that more of your boss's work?'

'Sure. We ran a fake building combine for that job. We built the movie palace with cheap rotten stuff, and we cleared up nearly a million dollars on the deal. We hired the men to do the job, and wound up the company the minute it was finished. When it did collapse there was no one to pin anything on to, except the official inspector who we bribed to pass it as safe and fireproof. How'd you like that?'

10

There was silence in the room for what seemed like minutes, while the kingpin looked me up and down. Then he spoke; and his voice, although it had lost the metallic tone imparted to it by the telephone that first time, was still recognisable to me.

It was disguised, of course; but perfectly. Every inflection, every tone and cadence had been studied out, and was strictly adhered to. The Raven said:

'Good evening, Barney — Leather. Good evening, Miss Beesly. How do you do, Mr. O'Halloran?'

'I was doing fine until your thugs got me,' I told him.

'Hmm-huhmm,' he chuckled, in a soft, sinister way, and in spite of the toughness you, pick up as a reporter, I still felt tremors shoot along my backbone. 'I'm sorry Barney and Leather worry you. But you won't be encumbered much longer

139

with their presence.'

'What do you want with me?' I snapped.

'Want? Only to put you out of the way, O'Halloran. You had a fair warning and you chose to ignore it. I haven't any intention of letting your futile little paper go to press again; and for that reason I am compelled to have you murdered. But first . . .'

I said: 'If you think I'm telling you anything, you're screwy.'

'It's only a simple question: just how much do you know, and how much of your knowledge have you imparted to others than your office staff?'

I shut my trap and kept it shut. He said:

'Come! Don't be sulky, Mr. O'Halloran. Don't let us have to coax it from you. How much have you told?'

'Plenty,' I spat out. 'Enough to see you all fried.'

'That's an exaggeration, I think, isn't it? I feel certain in my own mind that you know very little, and that you've told less. But the little you have told may possibly be a stumbling block to us, so it is as well that we should know . . . now . . . ?'

140

'You'll get nothing out of me,' I grunted. 'My middle name being Clam.'

'There are methods of opening clams, Mr. O'Halloran. Not very pleasant methods, I admit, but effective ones. I'll give you one more chance to talk . . . ?'

I didn't.

'Very well. Leather . . . you may proceed.'

Leather proceeded, the misbegotten bastard! He hit me with the thong he held again and again, and I wouldn't harass you folks with describing it to you again. But not a word out of me did they get; I can be stubborn as hell when I like, and I liked then. Leather laid off at last, gasping for breath, and I slumped forward against the ropes, half-dead already.

'A tough case,' mused the Raven, throatily. 'Have a few minutes' rest, Leather, then try again.'

The dame got up. Said: 'Let me try!'

Barney snarled: 'Siddown and keep quiet, Gayna!'

The Raven said: 'Wait — do you believe you could make him talk, Miss Beesly?'

141

She slunk over and took a look at me. She said: 'Sure. I've got different methods to a man's. I'll try them . . . '

I took a squint at her face, at her figure, and at her hands. And I got a sudden conviction this wasn't going to be a pleasant interlude. The Raven croaked: 'Go ahead, Miss Beesly. Show us your wonderful methods!'

She came over, and I mumbled feebly: 'Send the kiddies out. This ain't going to be any sight for children!'

That dame did things which had me shrieking inside of two minutes. If I could've gotten my hands to her throat I'd have ripped her jugular out of her lousy carcass without a second's pause, and with no compunction at all. But I was tied, tied tight, and she had her way. Once even Barney said:

'Hold it — Raven, you can't let her . . . '

'Shut up,' snarled the Raven. 'He begged for something like dear Miss Beesly's giving him. Leave her alone.'

I gritted my teeth and stuck her terrible twisting and wrenching for three minutes;

but when she got busy with a lighted cigarette, I cried off.

'Hell! Hold it — stop her! I — I — I'll talk.'

The Raven snapped: 'Good. Leave him alone now, Miss Beesly.'

The dame looked disappointed, but backed away. She knew better than to argue, even though she had been just beginning to enjoy herself. The Raven said: 'Thank you, Miss Beesly. Your methods are very effective; but, I fear, a little too cold-blooded for a mere male to put into practice. And now, Mr. O'Halloran — it's your move, I think?'

I squirmed and panted to ease myself. I said: 'I know very little, and what I do know I haven't passed on. It was all going into the next edition of the *Bombshell*.'

'There won't *be* any next edition,' said the Raven. 'Carry on with your remarks.'

I licked my lips, said: 'My throat's dry — maybe I could have a drink of water?'

Barney went out at a nod from the Raven; the Raven went on talking mockingly while he was gone, and I personally was thinking over how the hell

I could get out of this scrape. I didn't see any way. This was *so long*, far as I was concerned. I wondered if anyone would take over the *Bombshell*. Maybe Jimmy . . .

And suddenly there was an altercation outside of the door. Three voices, one of them belonging to Barney, were raised in argument.

'I tell you, he ain't back there,' barked Barney. 'Nobody's back there but me and my dame.'

'And we tell you he is,' came a second voice, and it was with a feeling of hopefulness that I recognised it as the voice of one of the detectives I had ditched outside. He went on: 'We saw him hit the deck and we saw him carried down here, soused. We've been waiting nearly an hour, and now we want to know what happened to him. If he's ducked out on us again . . . '

Barney repeated: 'Yeah, that's it. He ducked out the back way when he came too — yeah, sure he did. He'll be home by now.'

'We'll take a look just the same . . . '

Barney bawled: 'Hold it! If you try to shove your way through here, you'll be sorry. The guy who owns this place is a friend of . . . '

'We know, a friend of the chief of police. Okay, we'll risk it. Step aside.'

'I warn you . . . ' said Barney; then there was the sound of someone being pushed roughly away from the door, and one of the cops said: 'And *stay* out of it!'

The Raven hissed: 'The light!'

Leather slithered across the room, clicked the light switch.

The Raven muttered: 'We'll have to shoot them down . . . '

The door was being scraped open; light from outside filtered in; a narrow oblong on the floor gradually lengthened and extended each way. And I yelled: '*Look out*, fellers! They're *gunning*!'

The two dicks threw themselves back just as orange flame spouted in the gloom, and lead spewed out at the door. The Raven rasped: 'Blast you, O'Halloran! Here's *yours*!'

I threw myself and the chair backwards as he fired, and the slugs whistled past my head in the darkness. Then the door he had entered by was slammed suddenly;

two figures crammed into the room; there was further gunplay during which I hugged the floor. Then a wild scream, throbbing through the small room, a shriek of unutterable torment, like the wailing of a soul from hell . . . and then silence!

The light went on; the room was devoid of anyone besides the detectives, and a blood-soaked, huddled figure in the corner. A figure in a green dress, rucked up pathetically to show the white flesh and the fancy garters beneath. The figure of Gayna Beesly. One of the dicks put out a foot and turned her over; her face was a bloody mess where slugs had furrowed and ploughed into her skull. Her red hair was redder than ever. And she wouldn't ever do the things she'd done to me to any other guy — ever again.

I called: 'The guy you argued with at the door — get him. He's a killer.'

One of them rushed out again while the second untied me. The birds had flown; a search through the door they'd left by showed they'd gone completely, never to return. The Casino Club would have to get along without its lords and masters, or else close down.

Barney had beat it the front way; Leather had gone with the Raven; Gayna had gone all alone.

And me? I was still alive, somehow!

* * *

The D.A. wanted to know a hell of a lot; and although it was me who'd been through it in that room, the other papers scooped my own rag on it. But I wasn't worried. They didn't say too much about the why and wherefores; they were still acting under orders of their owners, who thought the Raven was best left alone. So it fell to the *Bombshell* to blow open the whole works, and it did. I used the front page to describe exactly what I've described above for you folks. I made a splash of it.

WHO IS THE RAVEN?

And I sent it along to the printers on press day, confident that when it was published two days later, it would sell to the last copy.

Which it would have done, only . . . well, let me tell you about that:

I was at the office late; checking over some of Jimmy's stuff. I was feeling tired, because it was only a few nights since I'd had myself a time of it in that Casino Club at the mercy of the Raven. The phone rang, and I wondered who could be calling so late; a sudden fancy told me it was the Raven, and I grabbed the receiver. It wasn't, though; it was Harry Salvo, manager of the Endor Printing Company on the line. He said:

'Larry? This is one hell of a mess you've got me into!'

'I don't get it? Something wrong with the copy?'

'*Plenty* wrong with it. *It's just got half the place blown sky-high; that's all!*'

I nearly dropped the receiver. Said: 'But how . . . ?'

'I'm just getting to that. I had a letter tonight. It read: 'Don't go to press with the *Bombshell*', and it was signed 'the Raven'. I laughed at it, asked myself what the hell he could do about it anyway, and went to press! We were just starting, when — *WHAM!* — a clutch of pineapples come sizzling through the window right on to the big press.

'We all ducked; when we got up again there wasn't any big press any more, just a hell of a mess of twisted ironwork! And two of our guys were badly injured.'

'Hellfire, I'm sorry, Harry. Listen, I'll be right down!'

I got right down; like Harry had said, the presses nearest the back windows were in a hellish state. Certainly they wouldn't be printing anything for a long time to come. Harry was standing by the side of a police investigator, spilling his heart out. All the wind seemed to have been taken out of him; he looked listless and tired, and there was an ugly gash right across his cheek where he'd been hit by a flying fragment of metal. When he saw me he said:

'As of tonight, you take your custom elsewhere, sonny boy.'

I patted his shoulder, answered a few questions that the cops put to me, and then drew him aside.

I knew I was going to have the argument of my life, but I meant to bring him over or talk myself unconscious in the process. I got all my forces mustered, then I said:

'Someday they'll erect a statue to you and your boys, Harry.'

He said, dismally: 'For what?'

'For *what*? Why, for carrying on and turning out the paper after all this has happened! That's what for!'

He turned away, pulling my hand loose off his shoulder. He said:

'I always thought they should have certified you, Larry. If they need anyone to sign you in, I'm the man. If you figure I'm sap enough to want to get myself blown up again, you must be crazy.'

I hauled on the tails of his overall and pulled him back. He swiped at my hand and said: 'Leggo, you damn fool.'

'Listen, Harry, you *got* to turn the paper out. It's in the best tradition. Think of what you'll be doing for your town, too.'

'That won't console me much when

I'm down among the dead men, will it?' he cursed. 'Besides, the press is gone. There isn't another big enough to turn your sheet out. Why don't you get your own printing works like a decent paper, then you could do what you liked? And take my tip — house it in a bombproof building!'

'Look, Harry — you wouldn't run out on me now, would you? I offered you the printing contract first before anyone, didn't I?'

'Sure you did. Because you knew I was sap enough to help you out when no one else would. I only run this place, you know. I'm answerable to the owner. I can't . . . '

'Please, Harry. I can't tell you what it means to me to get the edition out . . . you've got a spare press down below . . . use that . . . '

'It wouldn't run to the size. Only takes six-by-eight.'

'Then run it on that. You'll be safe in the basement.'

'Means a whole lot of setting — '

'I'll stay right here and alter the copy

— just so long as you turn it out.'

He was weakening. He said: 'The men won't want . . . '

'Tell them they get double time if they turn this out for me. I'll pay that!'

He made one last stand: 'But Larry, you know there's other work to be done. We're supposed to rush the *Manhattan Magazine* through for Saturday.'

'You can crowd that in somehow. If you can't, farm some of it out to another company. You can do it, Harry! You *will* do it! You wouldn't back out on a contract, no matter what . . . '

He scratched his head; he said: 'I'm a sap.'

He flung me some copy, said: 'Start altering that fast. Let the compositor have it when you're through. I'll have a chat with the boys.'

I got working on the copy. I worked like hell, and within an hour I had it ready for the machines. It was rough, but it'd do all right. I sent it through and stood around and watched while the boys went into action. The promise of double time had made them give their jangled nerves a miss; and now there was a police guard standing at every door, and two cops patrolling round the building.

Before I left, it was early morning; but the presses were rolling, and in my pocket I had a pocket-sized edition of the *Manhattan Bombshell*!

The Raven had been beaten once again. Now nothing could happen; tomorrow the edition would be rushed round to the distributors, and the day after, vans would peddle it all over the city. The rest could be safely left to the townsfolk to take care of. I knew they'd buy it in their thousands, like they had done the first issue. It might be different in size, but it wasn't different in content. It still carried a whole lot of pure dynamite!

I reached my apartment soon after the dawn had broken. I hadn't eaten for eight hours, and I had a large hole where my guts had used to be. I rooted through the icebox, got myself some salami, and washed it down with coffee and cream.

It made me feel better, and I was in a cheerful frame of mind when I finally climbed into bed. Nothing to worry about now; everything was swell. Far as I was concerned, the second edition was on its way; I hadn't anything to worry me except the sales, and I felt sure I wouldn't be let down.

It was nearly three in the afternoon when I awakened.

The phone was buzzing away in the other room, and I trod out to it in my pyjamas. It was the office; Valerie was on the other end, almost in tears: 'Larry . . . oh, Larry, get down here! Something *awful* is happening!'

11

Valerie was looking cuter than ever, except that there were lines of stress and worry under her eyes. I knew, although she hadn't said a lot, that she felt the strain of getting the *Bombshell* out as much as I did, that it had become as much a part of her own life as it was of mine, and that she worried like hell about me personally, where I was, and what I doing, and was I all right.

I couldn't have asked for better help than she and Jimmy gave me; of course, Jimmy's tasks were routine items, and didn't lay him open to any danger, but I knew if I was ever in collision with a brace of bullets he'd take right up where I'd had to leave off. I'd fixed it that way with him.

The second I came in Valerie came over and got hold of my arm.

'Larry, I'm so glad you're here.'

'What's been happening?' I asked, staring round to see if anything had happened to the office itself.

'It's the news-stalls — half-a-dozen of them have been ringing me up in the last fifteen minutes — '

'Asking for orders?'

'No. Asking me if we knew a bunch of toughs are going round threatening to break their stalls right up if they stock the *Bombshell* tomorrow!'

This was a move I'd expected. And I reached out for the phone when a call came in. I unhooked and listened:

'This is Sid, Larry,' said the voice. I started. Sidney Glassmer, the distribution agent. I said: 'Yeah? What's biting you?'

'Do you know fifteen newsagents have rung me up today to cancel their quota of *Manhattan Bombshell*? Know why?'

'Yeah, I think I do. Some uglies are galloping round telling them what'll happen if they stock the sheet tomorrow. But what can we do about it?'

'I was going to ask you that very same question. I've got seventy-five thousand copies over here, but if this cancellation of orders goes on much longer I won't even need five!'

'Stick to them,' I told him. 'I'm on my way round now. If any more news-sellers call, tell them I'll guarantee them protection if they take their quota. Hell, no one can do this kind of thing in Manhattan today!'

I slammed down the phone, grabbed it up again and dialled. I got through to the chief of police. I said:

'You know a band of thugs are hiking round threatening to tear people apart if they stock the *Manhattan Bombshell*?'

'Yes, we've had complaints.'

'And what are you planning to do?'

'What can we do? If any incidents are reported tomorrow we'll do our best to protect the person concerned.'

'Is that all? How about stationing a cop at each and every stall that stocks the *Bombshell*?'

'Don't talk drivel, O'Halloran. The force wouldn't run to it, you know it wouldn't. We can only hope for the best, and if we get the worst, do our best.'

I hung up with a snort. There wasn't a whole lot of help to be had there. I went round to Glassmer and got a list of the cancelled orders. I started out to each individual stall to see what I could do about it. Some listened to reason, some didn't.

'Sorry, I value my living too much.'

'It isn't worth it for what I'd make on the *Bombshell*.'

'No, do I want to be a martyr? Why should I?'

'Go peddle you own paper, son.'

And on the other hand:

'Sure, if you put it like that, son, okay. Send 'em along.'

'I'll take a chance. The usual fifty.'

'The cops won't be much use but, okay. You win.'

'Sure, I'll sell them. For jeez sakes, this is supposed to be a free country, ain't it? Sure I will.'

'No thugs are going to scare me.'

But the fact remained: at the end of the day, a matter of forty-odd orders, involving a total of twenty thousand copies of the paper, had been cancelled. But was I licked? Like hell.

I got back to the office and phoned a male employment agency pronto. I got through before the joint closed and had a word with the manager.

'Listen — it's imperative that I have a hundred men round, at the Glassmer Distribution Agency, early the morning.'

'What was the nature of the work?' asked the guy at the other end.

'I want them to sell newspapers,' I told him. 'It'll only be a day's job, but it'll pay off. Salary and commission. I don't care how you get 'em as long as you do. And there'll be a cut for you if you fix it.'

'A hundred's rather a tall order — but . . . I'll do my best.'

I hung up; I'd done all I could. Nobody could have done more. And, struck by a sudden suspicion, I ambled out of the office and set off for the Glassmer's Agency warehouse.

It was more luck than anything else that led me to stop off at the corner stall for an evening paper. I was eyeing them over and reading the headlines when two guys walked up. Two of the ugliest guys I ever saw, with mufflers and blue jowls. They looked along the counter, then one said:

'Got a copy of the *Manhattan Bombshell*, bud?'

The lame man who ran the stall bobbed his head apologetically.

'Tomorrer, mister. They don't come in 'til tomorrer. Save one for you if you like?'

'That's all we wanted to know,' said the spokesman. 'You *do* stock them, eh? Show him what's what, Spike!'

The other ugly walked casually around the stall while his pal kept a lookout; they hadn't noticed me behind a hanging wire frame full of magazines. I stood dead still.

The seller was backing away; the street was pretty quiet just there. He said: 'What's the game, mister? You didn't ought to be behind here, you know.'

The thug got closer up to him; said: 'If you stock any copies of the *Bombshell* tomorrow, you get your stall wrecked. Cancel your order, savvy?'

'Here,' blustered the seller. 'What the hell . . . *ouch*!'

He said that as the tough's knee shot into his groin, sending him off-balance. A hard, open hand flattened against the side of his face, and he gasped.

And just about then I'd jumped through into the stall.

The seller had sunk his teeth into his attacker's leg; he was a game little guy, but he made his mistake there. I couldn't reach him in time to stop the thug's foot battering into his face. The man jerked like a slugged rat, then lay still. I got my hands round the big boy's throat from behind, used a Judo trick I'd picked up, and sent him sailing over the counter to crash on his skull on the other side. His buddy was closing in fast, working his fists like a couple of pistons. I shoved my foot up as he came and caught him in the groin, a kick that stopped him like a stone wall. Then I fisted him smack on the snoot, and he reeled backward, not knowing which hurt the most — his snitch or his guts. But I wasn't through. This was something I'd been longing for. All the temper I had boiled over — I could almost feel it flooding out of my ears! I'd make a hospital case out of the swine or know the reason why!

He was on his knees as I rushed at him, and I could see the fear in his eyes; then my knee cracked against his chin, and his skull flew back, almost snapping his thick neck. I kicked him in the left ear for makeweight, and he fluttered down beside the paper-seller.

I went round to his pal, who was lying where he'd fallen with a split skull, surrounded by a little knot of sightseers. A cop arrived on the scene, and there was some hectic argument before he believed I'd only been defending what was right. The bookseller came round during this and weighed in with his evidence.

I watched the ruffians carted away to the station, then I flagged a cab and took the injured seller to hospital for emergency treatment. His pan was an awful mess, and when they were through he was one headful of bandages. Where he wasn't bandaged he was bruised plenty. I got a sudden idea, and asked him if he'd do me a favour. He said he would, and I took another cab.

We got out at the Press Club, and we walked right in. There were about thirty boys from various papers there; most of them I knew. I got up on a table and shouted for silence. I stood the seller — whose name naturally couldn't be anything else but Joe — up beside me. Someone gave an ironic cheer.

'This isn't an occasion for laughing, fellers,' I began, looking them up and down. 'This is serious. First of all I want you to meet Joe . . . '

There were calls of: 'Howdy Joe . . . '

'Which truck hit you, son?'

'Maybe the guy ain't got a face at all.'

I gazed at them contemptuously, and they suddenly saw the stare in my eye and resumed order. I went on: 'I'm not going to introduce you mugs to Joe, on account of he's a swell guy, and he wouldn't want to meet up with a bunch of sneering rats and dopes . . . '

'Take it easy, O'Halloran.'

'Yeah, I said *rats* and *dopes*, and I mean that. If you can see anything funny in a guy getting his pan mauled up, then I'd sure like to know *what*! This is one of the boys who sells your news sheets! You couldn't operate without him, there'd be no one to sell what you write. He's just as much a part of the press as you stinkers are . . . ' I was laying it on; I knew it was the only way I'd make my point.

People are like that — tell them pretty things about themselves and they'll get bored. Give them a few choice names to chew on, and they'll begin to wonder if you're right by any chance, and start in examining all the good deeds they could have done and never did. I went on:

'You had a good laugh at Joe's pan just now. But under that bandage Joe's suffering plenty. Oh, no, he wouldn't say so, that isn't his nature. You boys'd go whining all over the city if you stopped what I saw Joe stop tonight. But Joe doesn't. And now I'll tell you how he got that face . . .'

They were quiet now; I'd landed them. I pushed on:

'He got that face kicked in — *because he wasn't going to let anybody tell him what papers he'd sell and what papers he wouldn't sell!* That's why! He was told to cancel his order for the *Bombshell* — *he refused*.'

The sneaky Dave Golman said: 'The *Bombshell*'s your paper, O'Halloran. I hear you're having trouble with it — if these paper-sellers get tangled in your affairs, they should know what to expect.'

I rapped: 'What the hell does it matter what paper it is? Joe'd do the same for *your* papers if you were in the same spot. Suppose somebody didn't want your rags publishing? Suppose he had his way about it? *You'd all be out of jobs.* How'd you like that? And anyway, this is bigger than just *one* paper. The whole power of the press is at stake. Are you runts going to sit on your bottoms and have all your best stories squashed, and get told what to do and what not to do, by *someone you don't even know?* You know what I'm working for; you know. Jimmy Edwards is in with me. When I do what I set out to do, you'll all be able to turn in *any story you want.* Nobody'll dictate.

'But meanwhile, little helpless guys like Joe are going to get beat up all over town if they sell the *Bombshell*. Most of them'll take the chance — they won't be trodden on. But maybe it'll mean their stalls'll be busted up, their stock'll be ruined. At the same time you boys'll sit in the copy room and scratch your behinds! But Joe, and guys like Joe, will go right on selling what they want to sell, *no matter what*!'

I'd got them uncomfortable, that was plain. There were one or two murmurs, and some shuffling. I said:

'How about it, Joe? Are you intending to cancel your order for the *Bombshell*?'

'No, mister, I *ain't*,' said Joe. 'I got this bust leg in the last war, fighting Jerry. What'd be the use of it if was to allow myself to be ordered round and dictated to in my own country that I fought for? No, I guess I'll take all they can dish out, but they won't tell *me* what to do — the only way they'll get any satisfaction out of me is by putting me out of the game! That's a fact — I ain't just talking big. I *feel* like that!'

A silence followed; broken by Golman's sneering voice: 'It's a fake. O'Halloran put him up to it!' Somebody stamped. He yelped: 'Hey, who jumped on my toe?'

One of the other boys murmured: 'Shut up, Golman. I know Joe. He's a square guy — he doesn't double — deal for anybody.'

I said: 'That's the lot. I just thought I'd have Joe along and let you lugs see what a swell little guy he is — and don't forget there're dozens like him all over the city, who're going to get badly hurt when they start selling the *Bombshell*.'

Somebody said: 'What's behind this, O'Halloran? Give it to us? What can *we* do about it?'

This was it; I held my breath, then said: 'I'm going to hire a fleet of fast cars tomorrow morning. If these boys have guts enough to risk their necks, I'll spend all the mazuma I've coined so far to protect them as good as I can. But I need men to man the cars. The cops can't do everything. I need guys like yourselves, who haven't any morning assignments, or can skip them. I need you armed with coshes or any handy weapons. If there're any stalls broken up tomorrow, there'll be some heads to match them. That's what I'm asking for here — volunteers. And I don't want any lily-livered skunks, either.

'Anyone who's interested can see me at Glassmer's Distribution Warehouse tomorrow morning at seven. That's all, boys. Good night!'

And I gave Joe a hand and got right

down and walked out without waiting for an answer!

I took Joe home in a cab and dumped him. I said: 'Don't worry, Joe. You've had your share anyway. Tomorrow you'll find two husky cops to watch your stall while you sell the *Bombshell*. I'll see to that for you. So long.'

He said so long, then I got round to Glassmer's.

★ ★ ★

Sid was waiting there for me. The warehouse was closed; except for a night-watchman, everyone else had gone home. I took him aside and outlined my suspicions to him.

'It's this way, Sid — I've an idea the Raven'll do his damnedest to crash in here tonight — if not the big boss himself, then some of his mob. The plan'll be to destroy all the copies of the *Bombshell* you've got stacked up. If they can do that, they'd break me, since I need the dough the paper'll bring in. I couldn't afford to lose an entire edition that way.'

'And what do you want to do, Larry?'

'Stay here. Let the watchman do what he generally does, keep patrolling round the joint. But I'll be inside, and if anyone does try anything, *I'm* on the spot. Get me?'

He nodded: 'Want me to stay along?'

I considered that. Then said: 'Yes, it might be as well. If they make an attempt I don't expect they'll send more than two men along. Too many crooks spoil the broth in a case like this. We should be able to handle any corners between us all right.'

He said: 'I'll tell Henry to go about his duties like as always. We can stick back of the piles of the *Bombshell*, keep our glims skinned from there. Okay?'

We settled down behind the stacks, labelled ready for sending out in the vans the following day. Time dragged past slowly, and I begin to nod drowsily against the stack in front of me.

I woke up with a jerk in response to Sid's tug at my arm. He said: '*Quiet!* Someone's moving in here, and it ain't Henry!'

12

He was right; from the back of the warehouse could be heard a stealthy sound: slow, furtive steps, dragging along towards the stacks of *Bombshells*.

We stayed in cover; and heard a voice:

'Where's th' watchman, Barney?'

'He's okay. He's at the front of the joint someplace. Get the petrol, Leather!'

I gripped Sid's arm hard; the word *petrol* had told me what I wanted to know — the lugs were going to try and burn out the copies of the *Bombshell*!

They could, too; soused with petrol and set alight, those piles of dry paper would be blazing fiercely before anyone could hope to even get to them. They'd be gutted, and nothing would be left but a mass of charred paper and a razed warehouse!

Sid was as agitated as I was; suddenly I felt something pressed into my hand, and realised it was a small, trim revolver. I eased to my feet, and Sid eased with me. We started to sneak round the stack.

Halfway round, we could see the beam of a dimmed torch, and Leather sousing the front stack with juice. Barney was lighting a match; I could hear it scrape on the box.

We got out with a spring. I yelled: 'Grab air!' and then a whole lot of things happened at once. Barney streaked for his gun with one hand, and with the other flipped the hissing match into the petrol-soaked paper. There was a whoosh, and the front pile burst into flame with an ominous crackle. Leather had gone for his piece when I fired and knocked the torch out of his hand, shattering his fingers. The flames flickered over his gun as it came out, then I fired again and heard him yelp, his weapon clattering to the floor.

Meanwhile, Sid hadn't been asleep; I hadn't heard much from that quarter, except two shots . . . and glancing round out of the side of my eye, I was in time to see him lowering his revolver and Barney jointing at the knees, hitting the boards. I turned my attention back to Leather; he was streaking for the rear of the building as hard as hell.

I yelled: 'See what you can do about the fire, Sid. I'll get this rat!'

I started running as Sid groped out and got hold of an extinguisher. I loosed off two shots at a dark figure which was forcing through the open window at the back of the place, and missed. I ran on, got one leg over the sill, started to follow it with the other . . .

Wham! Something swished out of the shadows — a heavy piece of wood of some description — and caught me a filthy one across the side of the face. I threw lead in the direction it had come from, but nothing happened.

I got through and, too dazed to run, I stood there, swaying. The dizziness gradually wore off, and I began to think of Sid and the *Manhattan Bombshell*. I got back again as quick as I could, racing down towards the leaping flames at the far end, helping myself to an extinguisher on the way.

Sid and Henry the watchman were working like the devil, looking like a couple of characters out of hell in the red glow which spat up all about them. The first stack was blazing merrily; wasting no time, I got my appliance to work . . .

It was almost fifteen minutes before, with a sigh of relief, we laid aside our extinguishers and gazed sorrowfully at the mess. We were all covered from head to foot in white chemicals from the foam-spray, and our faces were blackened by flying specks and smoke.

But — the *Bombshell* was saved! And Barney was dead!

'Only the first stack gone,' observed Sid. 'About five thousand copies, that's all.'

'How about the foam — has it soaked through to the others?' I asked in trepidation.

He looked, then smiled. 'No. They're okay. Better get this wet mess shifted before it does, though.'

Henry got a mop and started slopping up the wet on the floor. I began scooping armfuls of the dirty, fire-gutted *Bombshell* up, and Sid pitched them into a clear space.

'Damn good job they were all roped together,' he stated. 'That made it harder for them to burn — if they'd been loose . . . '

We both raised our eyes to heaven; it didn't need much guessing to know what would have happened to them if they'd been in loose piles!

'Good job I had that hunch,' I said. 'If I hadn't . . . ' I shuddered to think of it. The edition would have gone up in smoke, and your favourite reporter would have been out of a job!

'We got a right to police protection now,' Sid said. 'I'll go phone the precinct.'

He did; inside of ten minutes four burly cops were on the spot, ready to do whatever we told them. We posted them outside, one at each set of windows, and one at each of the doors. Then we went back and surveyed the damage. There wasn't a great deal, but some of Sid's other stock had suffered a bit. I noticed a number of wooden cases to the right, somewhat charred.

'What's in those, Sid?'

'Those?' He looked at me peculiarly.

He whispered: 'Twenty gross of *celluloid dolls*!' and I nearly fainted!

'Hell! It's a damn good job we saved them — if the fire had just burnt through one of those packing cases . . . *ugh*! I'm sorry to cause you all this . . . '

He waved his hand. 'It isn't anything, Larry. Insurance'll cover any damage *I've* suffered. But I'm glad we saved your stuff. It doesn't belong to me, and therefore my policy wouldn't have covered it. You wouldn't have got a red cent. Well, it seems to be safe enough now with cops round the joint. What say we go home and get some sleep?'

'I'm getting some sleep,' I told him. 'But I ain't going home! No thanks. I wouldn't leave these papers again if you offered to surround the joint with cops — I'll sleep right here on the floor!'

And I did!

★　★　★

I slept hard, and I didn't wake until Henry the watchman gave me a call at four-thirty. I roused myself, looked at my

175

wristwatch, and then got to my feet.

Things were bustling in the warehouse. In the yard behind stood Sid's fleet of six trucks, and about a dozen men were busy loading these up with copies of the *Bombshell*.

Sid himself, looking as unperturbed as ever, was directing the operations, seeing the right vans got the right loads and seeing no one slacked on the job. At last the vans rolled away, two cops riding with each van. I'd arranged that with the D.A., and he'd kept his word to me and seen that the chief of police sent the men along. I knew also that the patrolmen were going to keep a special look out that day for any newsvendors who ran into trouble. By the time the last truck got underway it was half-past five, and Sid and I headed into the office and took a cup of strong coffee. Then I did a bit of 'phoning. I got on to a hire car company, and was put through to the manager, who was another of my useful acquaintances. He agreed to let me have ten cars right away, and send the drivers along with them. I hung up, and by that time there was a crew of fellows outside in the yard.

Sid said: 'These guys claim to have been sent along by the West Street Agency. You ask for them?'

I went out to them and looked them up and down. They were a ripe collection of bums and hobos, some young, some old, and some medium. I stood on a box and shot words at them:

'You birds don't know what you're here for, do you? I'll wise you up some then. You all heard about the newspaper, *Manhattan Bombshell*?'

They all opened their traps and nodded.

'You know what's going on, you know what may happen to guys who go out today and sell it?'

About five of them started sneaking away towards the gate.

I hurried on: 'That's what the job it. Sell the *Bombshell*. And because it's a tough proposition, I don't want anyone who'll sling his copies into the Hudson at the first sign of trouble. I want men who can hold their own if they need to; to make sure you aren't attacked, there'll be

177

a fleet of armed cars patrolling the streets where you're selling. But the cars may not happen to be there when they come for you, so if anyone wants to back out, they can do so.'

Eight more started walking, and the others looked uncertain.

'Because it's such a tough offer,' I went on, 'I'm willing to pay you birds two bucks each to sell five hundred copies of the *Bombshell*. It isn't hard to sell, and you ought to have cleared your quota in an hour's time. On top of that there'll be a cent on each copy sold as commission — that's five hundred cents on the same number of copies — that makes seven dollars in all you can earn for about two hours' work. Now, what about it?'

About fifty of them pushed forward: 'I'm in, mister.'

'Me too.'

'For seven bucks, I'd sell pamphlets on temperance!'

'Swell,' I enthused. Fifty was plenty for me. To the others who still stood there uncertainly, I said: 'You boys can blow. The job's taken. You were too slow.'

They blew; and we started issuing the hobos with their quota of *Bombshell*. Each man was given instructions to take up a position beside one of the stalls which had cancelled its order for the paper the previous day. We'd hardly seen half of them out when the fleet of ten cars arrived. I lined them up in the yard; up to now, I didn't have anyone to man them, but I felt sure the boys wouldn't let me down — or would they?

They didn't. About ten past seven, six arrived in a bunch. There was Williams of the *Chronicle*, Slade of the *Recorder* (my old paper), Moe of the *Sketch*, Talbot of the *Mercury*, and a couple more I didn't know too good. I welcome them with open arms and conducted them to the front car. I said: 'Good of you boys to turn up. How come you ducked your assignments?'

Williams said: 'Tench of the *Herald* agreed to cover the courts for the bunch of us. We were all assigned to police court duty, and there wasn't any need for us all to go — so Tench suggested he should take a report for us all. The morning's ours, Larry.'

'You all got weapons?'

They produced them: 'Great!' I grinned.

Williams had a cosh; Moe had a chair leg snapped off short; the others had everything from an old Indian club to a thick piston off a press. They looked like they meant business, and I knew they were tough babies.

I loaded them into the first car, then turned round to greet some new arrivals. They started to come in then. All told, there were about forty arrived in the next fifteen minutes, to battle for the honour of the newspaper game. They mostly all brought weapons along, and for those that didn't, I had provided a number of useful lumps of scrap lead piping. I packed them into cars in fours, and at last everything was set up.

I felt like a general marshalling his forces; and no general could have asked for a finer bunch of boys!

I walked along the line, telling each chauffeur which district to patrol. I told him to take it easy and just meander along, up and round the blocks and back again, and I warned the boys to stay out of sight as much as possible. If they spotted anyone being attacked for selling the *Bombshell*, they were to come out, give the thugs hell, tie them up with some rope I'd placed in each car, and phone for the cops. Then they had to get on with their beat.

That done, I took the first car myself, with Sid, Henry, and two cops. We started . . .

Everything was nice and peaceful; it was still early, and as yet the businessmen hadn't joined the early workers hurrying on their ways. As we went through Times Square, a clock face showed seven-thirty — and now, any minute, the rush would increase, the pedestrians already out would be joined by swarms of city men, on their way to the office, from Grand Central, from across the river, Brooklyn and Bronx, and as far out as Westchester County.

Midtown Manhattan was swarming by the time we arrived; now the other cars had broken off to go their separate ways, and we were on our own. At every news-stall we passed, the *Bombshell* was selling like wildfire. Men were bustling along the street reading the latest details of the Raven and his activities, and paper-vendors were rushed off their feet supplying the sheet.

Still no sign of trouble.

We got into a quieter district; there was a wooden shack at the end of the street where papers were sold. There was a display bill advertising the *Bombshell* right outside. Odd pedestrians were halting to purchase a copy, but business wasn't as brisk down here.

Then they came; just like that!

They came out of a side street, and they came fast.

There was about four of them: ugly, tough hooligans, looking for trouble. East Side guys.

They didn't do any arguing. They swept all the sheets off the counter on to the floor. The proprietor came hurrying round to remonstrate; he was grabbed by the neck, half-throttled, slung to one side, and then they began to push his stall over.

Our chauffeur speeded the car up and we bore down on them. We were still yards away when another car shot round the corner, screeched to a halt, and four of my reporters poured out. The way they whaled into those roughs was worth fifty cents admissions. In no time at all the burlys were strewn all over the roadway, marked and scarred with the impact of coshes and lead piping, and the boys were roping them into a neat bunch round a lamp standard.

We got out and helped; I said: 'Nice work. We were on our way ourselves.'

'This is our second,' grinned Williams. 'There's a bunch of three roped up two blocks away. The cops'll have them by now.'

'Who's going to press charges?'

'The stall proprietors will,' he told me. 'And be glad of the chance to get their own back.'

We rung the cops, then split up again. Five more blocks before we found anything else.

But this time it was a big street shop with an open front, and there were six wrecking it methodically. A cop was already trying to struggle with them and blow his whistle at the same time, and he was getting considerably the worst of it. We stepped up, swerved into the kerb, and piled out. Even the chauffeur got a loose wrench out of the seat and joined us.

It was hard while it lasted, but it didn't last long. The two patrolmen with us started in with their nightsticks, the chauffeur was cracking skulls right and left with his wrench, Sid was giving somebody hell with a heavy cosh, Henry was hiding in the back seat, and I was doing my bit of plumbing with a lead pipe . . .

Three minutes, and that selection of unwashed beauties were firmly roped round a lamp-post. There was one guy with them who stood out — he wasn't their cut. I hauled him to his feet, said:

'You leading this mob?'

'Not me.'

I slung him down again. We didn't have time to argue then, but I was pretty sure myself that he was no ordinary tough. He looked more to me like a regulation gang man, and the well-greased shooter which one of the cops extracted from his pockets said the same thing. We left them for the law, piled back in, and drove on . . .

13

At three o'clock that afternoon, as many of the boys as hadn't had to report for assignments turned up again at Glassmer's Warehouse. It had been a swell day, a great day. This issue of *Bombshell* had been cleared right off the stalls — there wasn't a copy to be had for love or anything else. In spite of all the trials, I'd kept my vow, and the second edition had gone through.

I'd have to start worrying about the third soon enough — but not for a while yet. Right now I planned to collect from the hobos we'd had peddling papers, go to see the chief of coppers and the D.A. about the toughs who'd been roped in, and then pick up Valerie and take in some show, preferably a musical comedy.

I felt good, and so did the boys who'd helped me. Sid was beaming all over his pan, and the reporters were looking like they'd done a good day's work, all pitching in towards an ideal.

Which they had.

Some of the hobos I'd hired never came back with the takings. But I'd expected that, and they'd only been an emergency measure. If I hadn't hired them, I'd have had some copies of the sheet left on my hands. At the same time, at least three-quarters of them did hand in their jack and take their pay, and to one or two who'd been mussed about a bit by the thugs, I paid a bonus of five bucks. I told them maybe I'd need them again in a week's time, and they all said they'd be okay for then. Then they skated.

Next I thanked the reporters personally, one by one, and told them what a great job they'd done. The most of them said they'd be around again next week, if I needed them and they could make it. They left too. At last, only Sid and I and his workmen were standing there. Sid looked at me, and I looked at Sid, and we both grinned.

He said: 'It's civil war, that's what it is!'

'Sure — but with swell fellers like that, we'll win!'

I left him tending his business and got along to the D.A.'s office. He had information in plenty for me. He said:

'You phoned us and told us the well-dressed toughs we picked up most likely had a hand in the Raven's gang?'

'That's right. You grilled them?'

'Yep. They don't know nothing about the Raven. They used to take their orders from Barney, but this morning they took them from Leather. That means, now Barney's dead, the Raven's using Leather for his mouthpiece.'

'What else did you find out?'

'Not a thing. Just that with each bunch of hoodlums there were one or two members of the gang proper.'

'Then the toughs weren't gangmen?'

'No, seemingly not. They're mostly East Side street corner loungers who were roped in at ten bucks a time to do their stuff under the direction of one of the gang boys. We did find one thing out, though — namely, that we've bagged all the gang proper except Leather and the Raven. They were all out on this job, and we've got the lot.'

I felt pretty good at hearing this: with his mugs gone, and only the thick-headed Leather for a lieutenant, the Raven didn't stand so good. The only thing I was afraid of was that he'd do a quiet bunk now, and desert the sinking ship. That, only time would reveal.

The chief of police shoved his oar in: 'What do you mean to do now, O'Halloran?'

'About what?'

'This paper of yours.'

'I don't get you, Chief — how'd you mean?'

'It's simple enough. You surely don't mean to publish a third edition after all this trouble?'

I handed him a frosty eye.

'I don't get you *yet*, Chief. You don't mean I should quit the game now, when we're sitting on the Raven's tail feathers?'

'That's just what I do mean. You're causing plenty of trouble. Why not leave us to locate your Raven for you now? Get out from under before the whole thing collapses on your head.'

'Leave it to you guys?' I gave him a hollow laugh. 'Don't say things like that,

Chief, you're killing me. This bird's been operating in Manhattan for five years, and it's my guess you never even heard of him until I brought it to your notice.'

He frowned, said: 'Don't get sassy, O'Halloran. If you aren't careful, I'll slide the skids under that paper of yours!'

I quit laughing. I glared at him. I snapped:

'You'll *what*?'

'You heard.'

'Sure I *heard*,' I snapped, 'and this I'll tell *you*: you try to do anything about stopping the *Bombshell* and I'll make you rue the day you set eyes on it! Get me?'

He stood up, angrily. 'Are you threatening me?'

'I'm *telling* you. What's wrong with you? Jealous?'

He snorted and stamped out of the office. I turned to the D.A.

'What's eating that guy?'

The D.A. grinned and said: 'You think he likes having your rag point out his pinches for him? Think I like it any more than he does? Only *I* don't mind how I get them, as long as I do — he *does* mind.

He likes the honour and the glory to go to *his* department. I'd advise you to watch your step with him, O'Halloran. He can get good and nasty — '

'Thanks, I will. And where do you stand?'

He shook my hand. 'Right alongside you. From now on, you can count on me for full support. It's thanks to you we've roped in a whole lot of bad men, some of whom we've wanted for months.'

That was something; and if I couldn't have the chief of cops alongside me, I'd settle any day for the D.A. and then some!

★   ★   ★

Valerie didn't waste any time with formal greetings when I breezed into the office just before closing time. She threw her arms round my neck and gave me a big kiss, and clung on until I got hot and bothered and had to push her away.

I said: 'How about you and me taking in a show? Got a pair of passes for the new musical at the Broadway. Like to see it?'

'With you,' she said, softly.

I grinned and gave her a peck. 'We'll want to eat first; I'm starving. We can go right now and eat, can't we?'

'Oh, I couldn't, Larry. Look at me — I'm only dressed for working.'

I did look; and to me, dressed for working or not, she looked pretty swell. But I'd thought of that. I said: 'There's a package on my desk. Go get it.'

She went and got it. She brought it to me. I said: 'That's by way of being a bonus for your help. Go ahead and open up.'

She looked at me, then started to untie the string. She got it open, and gasped. 'Oh, you shouldn't . . . it's *lovely*.'

It was a complete outfit for evening wear that I'd got her, right down to those things janes wear under their dress, and even shoes. It had cost some, but I was happy about the way we'd pulled the *Bombshell* through.

She threw her arms round my neck and kissed me. 'How did you know my size, Larry?'

'A guy picks things like that up in the

course of the day,' I told her. 'I had to make a guess at the size of the trunks and the bra, but I think it'll be near enough. Try it on, then we can get moving.'

She said: '*Here?*'

'Why, sure, where else?'

'But . . . '

'Don't worry about me — I'll go in the other office.'

'I wasn't worrying about *you*, Larry. But suppose someone came up?'

'Lock the door, then.'

She locked the door and started unbuttoning things. I got up to beat it inside. She said: 'You don't need to go, Larry. Just turn your head while I handle the more tricky items.'

*   *   *

The Broadway Theatre was jammed for the first night of the new musical *Lights of Hollywood*. It was a good show: lots of legs and lots of laughs. That happens to be what I call a good show, anyway, and you can take your critics and boil 'em. I enjoyed every minute of the first half, and when we headed out to the foyer during the interval, I was still laughing.

We sat down on a seat and grabbed a spot of pure air, and I had a smoke.

There was a guy next to me reading; I caught sight of the book first, a pocket edition of poems by Edgar Allan Poe. I glanced over, and saw he had the page open at 'The Raven'.

Now, maybe I would have thought nothing of all this, because there are many guys who like to read 'The Raven' over and over again, and I like doing it myself when I'm feeling morbid. But I happened to know this bozo, and several things added up in my mind. I said:

'Well, well, well, if it isn't Mr. Hammerton-Williams.'

He shut the book with a snap and glanced over at me.

He said: 'O'Halloran. I thought they'd certified you by now.'

'Not yet, not yet. In fact, I'm becoming quite a kingpin in the newspaper game, Williams. Or didn't you hear? I've got a good guy handling my distribution. On the whole, I'm glad you didn't take on.

Yes sir, really glad.'

He got up: 'I wouldn't be too sure of yourself, O'Halloran. If you ask me, you're walking right into a casket — and there'll be no printing presses inside that.'

'I wouldn't need a press where I'll be going,' I told him. 'It strikes me it'll be so hot down there, paper'll just burst into flames.'

He started walking away. Called back: 'I expect you're right about that. And it shouldn't be long now.'

'It shouldn't — maybe I'll see you down there, Williams . . . '

He was scarcely out of sight when I felt a tap on the shoulder. J.F. Meadle, that fat clunk I'd hired the office from, was leaning over and looking down at me.

'O'Halloran — '

'Well, J.F. himself. You'll be pleased to know your grand has doubled itself,' I told him. 'Before I'm through it'll have trebled itself, maybe more.'

He muttered: 'You're in too deep. I want the grand back. I'm bowing out. If they ever found out I was in with you, I'd get the same thing that's coming to you.'

I sat up. 'Which is . . . ?'

'You know the Raven'll get you sooner or later,' he stalled. 'Give me the dough back — send it to me. And take my tip and get out yourself before it's too late.'

I said: 'Get this, Meadle. You sunk your dough in of your own free will, and you aren't getting it out again now, see. The agreement we signed says I have the right to do what I like with it for the period of one year — and I'm sticking to it. If you want to crawl out, you lose the dough.'

He peered round as if he was afraid someone might be watching us. He muttered: 'Stick to it, then. But for God's sake, don't let anyone know I'm associated with the paper.'

'I won't, you lily-livered skunk,' I muttered as he slunk away.

I turned to Valerie with a laugh. I said: 'Everybody seems to think there'll be a big funeral in the city soon.'

'Is that what you were talking about?'

'That's it. I should rake off plenty in the way of flowers with all these nice guys so solicitous for my welfare. I extend an invitation to you to come along on the day and toss the first handful of dirt down . . . '

She shivered. 'Don't talk that way, Larry. It upsets me.'

I gripped her hand. 'Don't worry, baby. They've got to kill me before there's any danger of them burying me. And they won't manage that if I can help it.'

The music started up inside, and we walked slowly towards the swing doors. Going in, I bumped into Oswald Dexter, owner of the *Recorder*. There sure were a lot of folks I knew out tonight.

He said: 'This *is* a pleasure, Mr. O'Halloran. You're doing splendid work running this crook of yours to earth. I can see my investment is safe with you.'

'It is, O.D.,' I told him. 'It practically doubled itself.'

He nodded and looked at Valerie. He said: 'Aren't you going to introduce me to the lady, Larry?' jovially, rubbing his fat chin and smiling an oily smile.

I said: 'Why not? Meet the future Mrs. O'Halloran!'

14

'Well, well, congratulations,' said Dexter. 'You must be sure and let me know that happy day when you finally tie the old knot! I must send along a present for you.'

'That's okay,' I said. 'You don't have to bother.'

'But I insist — insist! And now the curtain's up, and I must be getting along to my box — I wish you both every happiness.'

He bustled off, leaving me looking after him with a frown.

Val said: 'He's quite a nice man, isn't he, darling?'

'A hypocritical old bastard,' I told her without mincing words. 'And yellow, too; scared of the Raven just like the rest of those bigtime paper owners.'

We saw the remainder of the show, and when we left Valerie suggested we should go to her apartment for supper. It was the first time she'd invited me up there. We went along, and while she busied herself with a number of tins, I flipped open a copy of *Liberty* and started to read the condensed novel there.

After we'd eaten, I got up. Valerie said: 'Going?'

I looked down at her. I said: 'I think I'd better.'

'Perhaps you're right. I'll see you at the office tomorrow then, darling. And don't be late.'

'Not now, I won't,' I chuckled. 'There's a big attraction down there for me from now on . . . goodnight, honey . . . '

She pulled me close to her and pressed against me. Her lips murmured against my cheek: 'Larry — promise me you won't take any more chances. There's me to think of now, besides yourself.'

'I won't. I'll do nothing in this case that isn't strictly necessary.'

I kissed her full on the lips, and she clung as if she didn't want me to leave her for a minute. But at last she let me go and I headed for the door.

'Night, darling.'

'Sleep well, baby.'

I took a last look; she looked cuter than ever standing there in the negligée she'd slipped into. Then I shut the door, lit a cigarette, and started walking homewards to help myself cool off.

I was too happy to hit the hay right away when I got in. I lay on the divan and stared at a photo of Val she'd given me, and wondered how she'd look in a cute nightie, sitting up in bed waiting for her husband. Her *husband* — *me*! Get that! Larry O'Halloran, guy without any pretensions to the features or physique of a screen lover at all.

What made dames like that go for chumps like me? Well, that's something I never will be able to figure out. But it was good enough for me to know that it was so; I didn't want to go into the whys and wherefores of it all.

I took a look at the shelf-clock. It read eleven-forty.

I felt maybe I could do with a snooze after the events of the day. It hadn't been an easy life on the *Bombshell* up to now, and the Raven was still at large.

I started to undress, draping my things about the room. I knew that was a habit I'd have to change when I got hitched. Women are funny about it.

I'd got down to my unions when the phone rang in the living room. I cursed and went out, treading gingerly on the cold lino in my bare feet. I lifted it, listened.

'O'Halloran? This is the chief of police . . . like you to get along to the morgue soon as you can — Elm Street morgue. We've got a body there you may be able to identify.'

'Body?'

'Young man, about twenty-eight to thirty. Only identification in his wallet was a scrap of paper with your office address on it. Can you get along?'

'Be right down.'

I slid into my duds again; I was tired, but this might be an item for the *Bombshell*. Why should any guy want to roam round with a scrap of paper containing my name and address on it? Or, rather, the name and address of the *Bombshell*.

I phoned an all-night cab service and

gave the directions; the cab dropped me off at the Elm Street morgue.

It wasn't a big place but it was plenty gloomy. There was an undertaking parlour on one side, and an ice cream company on the other. You could hear the refrigerators burring inside the ice cream factory . . . and I got to thinking that the contents of the fridges in that ice cream joint weren't any colder than the contents of the trays in the morgue — and not nearly as stiff.

The chief met me on the steps; he said: 'You're our only bet, O'Halloran. There wasn't anything else on him to check with. We picked him up down the Bowery tonight — er — you had your supper?'

'What's that to do with it?'

'Hem, have you?'

'Sure — had some lobster — tinned.'

'My God! Then you'd better make sure you've got a grip on your guts before you do this identification. Come on.'

That was the warning, but it didn't give me any idea of the actual gruesomeness of the thing I was going to see.

We headed down into the chambers

below street level, and went along past the rows of trays down there. The chief said:

'Where'd you put that murder case they hiked in tonight?'

The attendant studied his list, said: 'The poor guy with the face? Twenty-three, sir.'

We walked down to tray twenty-three; the chief grabbed the handle and pulled.

The tray slid out, neatly.

There was a formless mass underneath a white sheet.

He hauled the sheet aside . . .

I turned away after one glance. I said: 'You're right. It doesn't go well after that lobster. Cover it up, Chief.'

He covered it up. 'Know him?'

'Yeah, I *knew* him. He worked for me — routine crime reporter. Name was Edwards. Jimmy Edwards.'

'Poor kid — tough luck.'

I said, unsteadily: 'Got a cigarette?'

He gave me one and I lit it with a trembling hand. 'How'd it happen?'

'Must have been the brick we found beside him covered with blood. Somebody trapped him down a cul-de-sac and battered his face and head in with it.'

'Robbery?'

'No. We found fifteen bucks and some loose change in his jeans, and another thirty in his money belt. May have been a warning . . . '

'Some case he was working on for us?'

The chief shook his head. 'No; a warning to you and to your paper. We found this on him . . . '

He took a black feather out of his pocket. He handed it to me. I muttered: ''*Leave no black plume as a token*' . . . Hell!'

'What is it?'

'I guess my guess is the same as yours — it's the tail feather of a raven. Isn't that right?'

'That's right. What was it you said before, though?'

'It wasn't important. Just a piece of a poem called 'The Raven'.'

'Never heard of it,' grunted the chief, happy in his abysmal ignorance. 'What's a poem got to do with this?'

'Not a thing; except that I think that's where the killer got the idea of calling himself the Raven. And there were no clues, you say?'

'Not even the conventional button. But we can safely say this was done — or at least directed — by the Raven.'

'Yeah — sure. That's obvious. It's a warning, as you say.'

'Take my advice and heed it. Keep your nose out of this mess from now on and leave it to us.'

'No! You think, after this, I'll stand aside? Like hell I will, Chief. I'll get this bastard if it's the last thing I ever do.'

We went out to the street again. I was wondering how Valerie would feel about it when she heard. She'd liked Jimmy; he was good company for her. I knew she'd be damned cut up. I was glad she hadn't seen the corpse back there.

I decided I'd go right round and tell her about it. I said so long to the chief and started to walk. I walked slowly, not too anxious to get there and have to start telling her.

I went up to her flat by means of the automatic elevator, pressed the door buzzer. Could hear it buzzing inside, but no one came to answer it. I kept pressing, kept trying. I knew she'd be hurt if I didn't tell her what had happened to the kid right away. Besides which, I wanted sympathy myself. I felt pretty awful about it, felt it was my fault the kid had got his. And it was, whichever way you boiled it up and simmered it. It still added up to the fact that I'd bunged him full of my own ideals and he'd stepped in with me, not knowing what he might get as his share of the reward for doing so, but never thinking it would be a shattered face in a dark alleyway in the Bowery! And a cold slab in the Elm Street morgue.

Life went on all round, and Jimmy Edwards lay dead and cold in the heart of the city. Dead, and cold, and stiff — and I found myself clenching my hands and muttering over and over:

'The dirty bastard! I'll get him — I'll get him!'

I pulled myself together; still no one had answered that bell. A sudden fear leaped madly into my thoughts — suppose . . . suppose they'd treated Val the same way as Jimmy? Suppose she was lying inside there, her face . . . ugh!

I tried the door; it opened to the touch. I headed in. I went straight to her bedroom after switching the light on. That door stood open, too; I flipped the bedroom switch, stepped in, and stared round dazedly.

My first feeling was one of relief; whatever had happened, she hadn't been murdered here. But she wasn't in bed.

The bed had been slept in, that was plain. The clothes were all rucked up as if someone's legs had been kicking them about. Her underthings had fallen off a straight-backed chair beside the bed when it had overturned. A glass of water lay splashed about nearby.

I started getting panicky. I called: 'Val — *Val!*'

I went over to the bathroom and peered in there. Nothing. I came back with a rush and started racing foolishly round the room, trying to reassure myself that she had slipped out somewhere and would be right back. But I knew she hadn't. The bedclothes, to my touch, weren't even warm. She'd been gone a long time.

I grabbed the telephone and got through to the precinct.

'Send somebody over, and hurry,' I said. 'It's urgent. A girl's vanished, and I think the Raven had something to do with it.'

Then I sat down, a mass of jitters, with nerves a mile wide and raw at the edges, to wait for the law to get its ponderous wheels into motion.

It was a warm night, even hot, but I was shivering like a man with malarial fever when the cops arrived. I told them as much as I could, and before I'd finished talking we were joined by the chief. He said:

'All right, O'Halloran. Take it easy.'

'*Take it easy* be damned!' I howled, shaking my fist at him. 'I tell you, I know the Raven's got this girl. He must have. It all points to that explanation.'

'I know, I know. But it won't help you or the girl to lose your hair, will it?'

I groaned and subsided. He couldn't do anything more than I could myself.

Which was precisely nothing — nothing but wait, and hope.

And then one of the patrolmen said: 'What's this?'

We hadn't noticed it before; it was stuck in the top of her dressing table mirror, and it was black and long. The chief looked at it, then at me.

'That settles it.'

It was a black plume — another feather from a raven's tail piece!

'Take my tip: get to bed and have a good night's sleep,' said the chief as the police car dropped me at the corner of my block. 'Things will seem better tomorrow.'

I handed him a hollow laugh; I felt so bad I almost wished I was lying in that morgue along with Jimmy Edwards. Knowing what a cruel swine the Raven was, I was driven half-insane worrying over Val's safety. I swore that if and when I got my hands on him — I'd strangle the Raven personally, and take a long time about it.

But it wasn't any use thinking that way; tomorrow I wanted to be able to do something constructive towards getting her safely back, if she wasn't already beyond bringing back. And I didn't think she was. If they'd intended to kill her, why had they taken the trouble to smuggle her out of the building?

I turned into bed, but I didn't sleep. My whole body felt tired and ill, and my face was paining me from the innumerable hard knocks it had taken recently. I tossed and turned until the bedside clock told me it was turned four in the morning, then I got up.

I had a shave and shower and felt better; I forced myself to eat a plate of ham and egg, then wished to God I hadn't. I could feel it surging up and down in my guts, and it was only by a tremendous exertion of willpower that I didn't lose it.

The telephone rang.

'O'Halloran speaking,' I said, listlessly.

Then stiffened; a gloating chuckle had crossed the wire!

He started quoting, right off: "Prophet!' said I, 'thing of evil! — prophet still, if bird or devil! / By that Heaven that bends above us — by that God we both adore

— / Tell this soul with sorrow laden if, within the distant Aidenn, / It shall clasp a sainted maiden whom the angels name Lenore —

"'Clasp a rare and radiant maiden whom the angels name Lenore.' / Quoth the Raven, 'NEVERMORE'!'

He finished quoting, chuckled: 'The name isn't quite right, but the sentiments are, aren't they, Mr. O'Halloran? That's what you want to know, don't you? Will you ever see her again?'

'You swine . . . ' I yelled.

'Not so fast. We're very near the end of the poem now. You realise that, don't you? But I am not going to be as cruel as the raven in the poetry, Mr. O'Halloran. I am going to be merciful, and tell you that your chances of seeing your lady love are even — if you refrain from publishing the *Bombshell* and interfering with my affairs. Take your choice . . . and if you choose wrongly, it will be '*Nevermore*'.'

15

I gripped the receiver as if it was the Raven's neck. But I controlled my voice, said: 'What do you want me to do?'

'Do? Nothing; nothing at all. Just throw in the *Bombshell* and stop interfering. When I am convinced you are playing to my orders, the girl may be released.'

'And how about Edwards? Why kill *him*?'

'To let you see that I still manage to have my own way even if my gang is broken up. Leather did that. He could have knifed him, but Leather loves messy methods. Not very strong in brain, but very useful, is Leather. It was he who went for the girl tonight. Rather well done, that: he had, of course, to inject a drug into her — from which she has not yet regained consciousness, I fear — but that enabled him to convey her to the waiting car without any trouble.'

'Suppose I obey your orders? How do I

know I can trust you?'

'You have no choice. You must take the risk — and I'm sure any risk is justified to save the life of the girl you plan to marry, isn't it? Such a beautiful young lady, too. I feel sure you wouldn't disobey with her at stake.'

But I hadn't been listening to his last words. Suddenly, I knew everything; *who* the Raven was, *why* he was — and possibly I could soon find out *where* he was! It came upon me with startling clarity, and I *knew* I could not be wrong. Like most criminals, the Raven had made his slip!

I said: 'I'll do as you say. Don't harm her.'

'Have no fear of that. If you desist from meddling . . . '

'I won't meddle.'

He chuckled again, and there was a faint click from the other end of the wire. And immediately, I moved.

I got outside, boarded a trolley which would drop me off near a select part of the city. I found the place I wanted, a large and commodious house in its own grounds. The residents were not yet up, but I hammered on the doors until I got a reply.

An aged servant opened the door and eyed me with suspicion. I snapped: 'I wish to see your master urgently. Is he at home?'

'No, sir. He ain't been home for two or three nights.'

'Damn! Any idea where he might be?'

'I don't rightly know, sir. He don't like nobody to know 'bout his comin's an' his goin's. But I expect if it's very urgent . . .'

I showed him a fifty-dollar bill. I said: 'It's that urgent!'

'That is urgent enough, sir. He's got a small place down at Long Island. A little bungalow . . .'

He gave me the address, and I raced out again and got myself a payphone at the corner. I phoned a cab with orders for it to get to where I was, fast. It rolled along inside ten minutes, and I threw myself in the back, said:

'Long Island. I'll tell you where when we get there.'

He moved off, and I fumed and

fidgeted in the rear, bursting with impatience. Every second that passed I was becoming more sure; but I had to be really sure before I could phone the police. If I'd made a mistake, I'd find myself involved in the biggest court case ever to hit Manhattan!

We reached the island, and I said: 'Drop me here and wait for me. If I'm not back within fifteen minutes, call the police and tell them where I am, and that I've got the Raven — or he's got *me*.'

I didn't wait for his reaction; I started moving along the deserted roadway, hugging as much cover as was available.

I came to the bungalow called 'The Nest'. Yes, The Nest, the Raven — it was all in keeping with the fiend's melodramatic personality. I prayed the birds wouldn't have flown.

The bungalow lay back from the road, a couple of hundred yards from its nearest neighbour. The front door was closed, and the whole thing had an appearance of desertion and stillness. A sudden feeling that I was wrong, that I was acting the fool, came over me. I threw it off; I had to be right this time.

I started walking along the path, keeping to the shelter of a hedge of shrubs which just extended above my head. I got my hand on my gun, brought it out of my pocket, flicked the safety off.

Now for it.

To reach the window I had to sneak past the front door. And I was exactly halfway across the open space when the door opened, and *Leather stepped out*!

He saw me at the same time I saw him. Only I already had my gun out, and I wasn't waiting to argue. I pulled the trigger, twice, watched him grab his guts and go screaming to the dirt path front of the door. He squirmed about in torment, and I began to rush the bungalow.

Slugs ripped through the open doorway, tore bitingly into my left thigh. I fell almost on top of Leather himself. I lay there groaning, my gun having flown some four yards away when I had taken the fall. A man stepped out of the bungalow . . .

'The end of the poem, eh, O'Halloran?' he said, glancing up and down to see the place was clear of anyone else. 'So you couldn't stay out of it after all? Ah, well, I had meant to kill your bride-to-be anyway, and now you can go together.'

'I knew it was you,' I grated, between my teeth. 'I knew it when you made that slip on the phone . . . '

'Slip? Which slip?' he asked, puzzled, but keeping his gun trained.

'You didn't spot it, did you? Remember, you told me that Valerie was still senseless, that she hadn't recovered from the effect of the drug Leather gave her. So she couldn't have told you we were to be married, could she? And yet you knew! And there was only one living man who knew Valerie and I intended to get married. Only one person in the world, who I told myself last night in the interval at the Broadway Theatre.

'You see? *That* was your slip, Dexter!'

Oswald Dexter smiled. 'You're very perceptive. Yes, it was a bad slip. How did you find me down here?'

'Tried your home and got your address here from your servant. The minute you made that slip on the phone this morning, it all became clear. The only discordant thing was the five thousand dollars you advanced towards the *Bombshell*.'

He nodded. 'That was to avert suspicion from myself, just after I'd tried to buy you out. It did, didn't it?'

'It did. I never would have suspected you but for your phone call. You might even have got away with it.'

'I *will* get away with it,' he said in a sharp voice. 'Just as I always have done. Just like when I was at the head of the firm which supplied rotten food to the orphan homes. I've been at the heads of *several* other firms of the same type. It isn't that I need the money, O'Halloran. I have plenty. But I like the *power*. I like the sense of omnipotence it gives.

'I'm crooked by nature, I expect. But of course I didn't want to take any chance of being caught. Good heavens, no! When one of my own reporters on the *Recorder* went out and got that orphan asylum scandal, and my own editor printed it in my own paper, I decided steps would have to be taken to muzzle the press. You know how that was accomplished. I even wrecked part of my own premises for the sake of safety. After that, I had no trouble — until you decided Manhattan needed a new paper which wouldn't fall down on its job.

'I admire you, O'Halloran. I admit that. I admire your guts and your nerve, and the way you've put things over. If you'd listened to reason, I couldn't have wanted any finer editor for the *Recorder* than you are. But now you've missed your chance, I'm afraid.'

'You'll kill me?'

He nodded. 'And your girlfriend.'

I said calmly: 'Why kill her? What did she do?'

Dexter shrugged: 'I must. I couldn't risk letting her live now. She'd be too nosey — might even carry on the *Bombshell* for you. No, she must die — but she will know nothing. I will shoot her while she is still unconscious.'

He was watching Leather, whose squirming was growing feebler. His eyes were momentarily off me; he didn't expect anything from my quarter. Why should he? He knew my thigh was smashed, he knew my gun was yards away, he knew I couldn't have moved an inch with the agony which was making me bite into my lower lip.

He was watching Leather's face; and what he didn't see was Leather's revolver!

Leather had had it out when I'd got him. When he dropped, it dropped with him. Now it lay on the side of his body nearest me, concealed from Dexter by his arm. By sidling one hand towards it I found I could reach it easily. I got my fingers round it.

Dexter didn't even know it was coming. I gave him it all, seven shots, each shot ploughing deep into his lumpy, grotesque frame, each shot making him jerk and quiver. His gun slipped out of his hand; his eyes, glassy, found mine. He was wounded in seven places, and it was more his huge bulk keeping him upright than anything else. He murmured:

'O'Hall- . . . '

I said grimly: '*The end of the poem, Raven!*'

Then his lips twisted in a peculiar

smile, and he crashed forward on top of Leather!

★   ★   ★

'Feeling all right, darling?'

I grinned up at Valerie, and nodded.

It was eight days later. After Dexter had hit the earth, I had passed out myself. But the taxi driver had obeyed the orders I had given him implicitly, and after my time had elapsed had telephoned the police as directed.

It was only that which saved my life; otherwise I might have stayed there for hours undiscovered, and slowly bled to death.

It had saved Dexter's life, also. But only for a brief period. Word had been brought to me the previous day that Dexter had passed away in hospital.

That was the end of the Raven and his gang. Leather had died out there in Long Island from my shots.

Valerie sat on the edge of the bed, taking care not to knock my injured thigh. I said: 'About the *Bombshell* . . . '

'I've been so worried I haven't been

221

able to think of it.'

I nodded; couldn't expect the kid to think of it anyway, after what she'd been through. But it meant I was out of a paper!

She said: 'Feel up to seeing a man?'

'About what?'

'Oh, just a man,' she said mysteriously. 'He's waiting outside.'

I said: 'Okay, if you think I should see him.'

She went out and returned at once with a thin, beak-nosed specimen carrying a briefcase. He opened it, took out some papers, cleared his throat, then said:

'Hmm! I am Mr. Dexter's — I should say, the *late* Mr. Dexter's — legal adviser, Mr. O'Halloran.' He coughed again, said: 'I can perhaps explain best by reading to you a passage from the will of the late Oswald Dexter, dictated to me, in the presence of two witnesses, the day prior to his demise.' He looked important, started reading: '"And further, to Lawrence O'Halloran, late of the New York *Recorder* and now editor of the *Manhattan Bombshell*, I bequeath all my interest in the said newspaper, New York *Recorder*, so that he may run, alter, edit and adapt the said paper as he chooses, with one stipulation: that he must at once change its name to the *Manhattan Bombshell*.

''Thus do I attempt to discharge, in part, any suffering and loss which I have caused to him.'' The beaky man gazed at my astounded face, then said: 'He also finishes very strangely. He says: 'And my soul from out that shadow that lies floating on the floor / Shall be lifted — *nevermore*!' The Raven'.'

Dexter had stuck to his dramatics to the last!

We do hope that you have enjoyed reading this large print book.

Did you know that all of our titles are available for purchase?

We publish a wide range of high quality large print books including:
Romances, Mysteries, Classics
General Fiction
Non Fiction and Westerns

Special interest titles available in large print are:
The Little Oxford Dictionary
Music Book, Song Book
Hymn Book, Service Book

Also available from us courtesy of Oxford University Press:
Young Readers' Dictionary
(large print edition)
Young Readers' Thesaurus
(large print edition)

For further information or a free brochure, please contact us at:
Ulverscroft Large Print Books Ltd.,
The Green, Bradgate Road, Anstey,
Leicester, LE7 7FU, England.
Tel: (00 44) **0116 236 4325**
Fax: (00 44) **0116 234 0205**

THE MISTRESS OF EVIL

V. J. Banis

John Hamilton travels to the Carpathian Mountains in Romania, along with his wife Victoria and her sister Carolyn, to research the risk of earthquakes in the area. The government provides lodgings for them in the ancient Castle Drakul. Upon investigating a disused basement room, the trio discover a skeleton in a coffin with a wooden stake through its rib cage — and Carolyn feels a strange compulsion to goad John into removing it. Soon afterward, a sinister visitor arrives at the castle — claiming to be a descendant of the original Count Drakul . . .

THE GREEN MANDARIN MYSTERY

Denis Hughes

When a number of eminent scientists — all experts in their field, and of inestimable value to the British Government — mysteriously vanish, the police are at their wits' end. The only clue in each instance is a note left by the scientist saying they have joined 'the Green Mandarin'. Desperate to locate his daughter, Fleurette, a Home Office official enlists the services of scientific detective Ray Ellis. But as his investigations get closer to the truth, will Ray be the next person to go missing?